P9-DNJ-230

HAYNER PUBLIC LIBRARY DISTRICT
ALTON, ILLINOIS

OVERDUES .10 PER DAY MAXIMUM FINE
COST OF BOOKS. LOST OR DAMAGED
BOOKS ADDITIONAL $5.00 SERVICE CHARGE.

WINGS

WINGS

JULIE GONZALEZ

delacorte press

HAYNER PUBLIC LIBRARY DISTRICT
ALTON, ILLINOIS

Published by
Delacorte Press
an imprint of
Random House Children's Books
a division of Random House, Inc.
New York

Text copyright © 2005 by Julie Gonzalez
Jacket illustration copyright © 2005 by Michael Morgenstern

All rights reserved. No part of this book may be reproduced or transmitted in
any form or by any means, electronic or mechanical, including photocopying,
recording, or by any information storage and retrieval system, without the
written permission of the publisher, except where permitted by law.

The trademark Delacorte Press is registered in the U.S. Patent and Trademark
Office and in other countries.

Visit us on the Web! www.randomhouse.com/teens
Educators and librarians, for a variety of teaching tools, visit us at
www.randomhouse.com/teachers

Library of Congress Cataloging-in-Publication Data

Gonzalez, Julie.
Wings / Julie Gonzalez.
p.   cm.
Summary: Ever since he was a little boy, Ben, who wanted to be called Icarus,
persisted in believing that he would grow wings and would fly, a belief that
perplexed and worried his family and friends.
ISBN 0-385-73227-9 (trade)—ISBN 0-385-90253-0 (glb)
[1. Wings—Fiction.   2. Identity—Fiction.   3. Brothers—Fiction.
4. Flight—Fiction.]   I. Title.
PZ7.G593Wi 2005
[Fic]—dc22
2004007158

The text of this book is set in 12-point Minion.

Book design by Kenny Holcomb

Printed in the United States of America

April 2005

10 9 8 7 6 5 4 3 2 1

BVG

UF
GON

616759643

To Eric

ACKNOWLEDGMENTS

Thanks to Françoise Bui, my editor

And to my family

Surely he is mad; for what is a dream but a
dream, and a vision but a vision? They are not real things
that one should heed them.

From "The Young King," a fairy tale by Oscar Wilde

BEN

Even before I was born, I knew I could fly. I mean, I really *knew* I could fly. Like somewhere deep within my heart and soul lurked the magic of flight, and my task, my challenge, my life's mission, was to achieve flight. Not with machines, mind you. I wouldn't have gotten into some machine and claimed I was flying even if I was at the controls. Like if you're in a boat, are *you* floating or is the boat? Right . . . it's the boat floating. Without that boat you'd sink like a stone. So this was how I saw it—machines could fly, and people could operate machines. Two totally different things.

Let me tell you right off that I wasn't born with wings . . . not visible wings anyhow. Not even stubby useless ones that were surgically removed in the cold, sterile environs of some subterranean operating room. No. There were no under-developed little nubs poking from my sweet infant back. No extra flaps of skin connecting my arms to my torso. Nothing like that.

But I always believed I had wings. In fact, I can't tell you how many hours I spent in front of the mirror with no shirt on, searching for some sign of those wings. And, believe me, it's hard to see your own back in the mirror. You really have to twist yourself up, and if you stay that way for too long, it's miserably uncomfortable. I never saw any sign of those wings, though, no matter how hard I tried.

I decided I had some latent kind of wings, up under my skin, not yet emergent, so to speak, just snuggling in there morphing around till the time was right. Sometimes I thought I could feel them. They scratched at my skin from the inside. They wanted out!

There was something else I knew about my wings, something important. They weren't brightly feathered creations like those of birds. And any wings itching to hatch out of my back sure weren't an angel's wings. Anyone who knew me could've testified to that. Nor were my wings the tissue-thin, translucent, iridescent jewels some insects have. No.

My wings were reptilian.

You heard me. Reptilian. And I know what you're saying because I'm sure it's the same thing my brother N always used to say. "Reptiles don't have wings!" Well, just slow yourself down, because get this—dragons are reptiles and dragons have wings. So don't be in such a rush to discount my words.

IAN

My brother, Ben, who was seventeen the last time I saw him, is twenty months younger than me, but an inch taller. He has blue eyes like the ocean, and curly hair that is like my mother's wedding ring—yellow, but also gold. Ben is like fire—captivating yet unpredictable. He's smart, too. He can hear something one time and retain it for life. He never wanted to go to college, though. For Ben, higher education referred to altitude, and he said he'd achieve that when he got his wings.

Ben always did have the quicker mind of the two of us. He rarely cracked a textbook when we were growing up, yet the only thing that blew his GPA was that he never turned in his assignments. He said there had to be something better to do after school than homework, and the thing he was talking about was flying. From my earliest memories, Ben thought he could fly. I don't mean in a plane or anything like that. I mean like a bird. Or a dragon, to be truly accurate. It drove our mother crazy. She'd be in the kitchen peeling potatoes or cleaning fish, and out of the window she'd see Ben jumping from a tree or off the roof of the barn. She'd run out of the house trying to stop him, but she never reached him in time.

Ben must have been about a year old when he had his first major showdown with Gravity. He was such an innocent-looking little thing, with all these soft gold curls surrounding him like a halo gone haywire. Ben didn't learn to walk, he learned to run. Everywhere he went, those little legs would be going like the scissors of a manic hairdresser. Ben was always busy, always moving.

Usually we had baby gates at the top and the bottom of the stairs, but that morning my father had bought a second-hand chest of drawers at the flea market, so he removed the baby gates to get the chest up the stairs. To Ben, that was an invitation. He ran down the upstairs hall, flailing his arms like an angry chicken in a rainstorm. He ran right off the stairs, flapping his arms and pumping his legs, and tumbled all the way down in a noisy symphony of bumps and thumps. I stood on the landing, astonished at what my baby brother had just done. My parents came running: my father from the kitchen, where he was making lunch; my mother from our bedroom, where she was filling the new chest of drawers with our clothes.

"Ben," my mother cried out, and she raced down the stairs. By this point my father had scooped Ben from the floor and was cradling him in his arms. "Is he hurt?" my mother asked frantically.

"I'm not sure," said my father, using his thumb to brush the blood away from a cut on Ben's forehead. "Doesn't seem to be. Not seriously, anyway. Cuts and bruises."

Ben wasn't even crying. But he was furious. He kept saying, "Why didn't my wings work? Why?" Course my parents weren't sure what he was saying because they were so flustered, but I understood his babyspeak perfectly.

BEN

I remember when I was born. After nudging Mom a few gentle times from her dark, warm interior, I was delivered into the world. A healthy little full-term squawker, thrashing his arms. The midwife told Mom she'd never seen a baby thrash so! Well, of course I was thrashing . . . I was feeling for my wings. And I can tell you I was surefire mad that they didn't show themselves to me right off.

There N was, a serene, quiet little tyke sucking his thumb and looking at me like I was the devil himself! I don't suppose he was expecting me when Mom told him a surprise was coming along.

I asked N in baby language where his wings were, but he just kept chomping on that thumb. Must have tasted like chocolate milk or something. I saw him there and thought maybe his wings were underneath that extra skin he had on. It was actually his shirt, but I didn't know it at the time.

It took me a while to realize that my very brother had no wings. He used to get so mad at me when I prodded and poked at his back looking for them.

"Lie down, N, on your stomach. I wanna look at your back."

"What er ya looking for, Ben?"

"Yer wings." I rubbed his back all over, but I couldn't find any wings.

"Not again, Ben."

"Just lemme look."

"I don't have any wings, you dope. I'm a people, not a bird."

"They've gotta be here somewhere," I insisted, scratching at his skin.

"Get offa me, Ben. I tell you I don't have any wings!" He flipped me from his back.

I must have been about four the last time I looked for N's wings. By the time I started kindergarten, I knew N didn't have wings. But here's the weird thing about N—he never wanted wings. Not even a little.

BEN

Birds and insects made flying look so easy. When I was little, I watched them all the time, soaring up there in the sky. I liked to lie in the grass at dusk, and wait until the sky softly darkened. The flying things were always busy at twilight. The dragonflies would be dining on mosquitoes, which were so tiny I couldn't even see them. Bees would be buzzing around in some secret honeydance. Gnats and no-see-ums would tickle my eyes and nose. Small birds would be weaving around snatching bugs. Then the bigger birds would be swooping around, maybe on their way home after a long day.

But what really fascinated me were the bats. Every evening I would wait patiently for them to appear. They would dart in front of the other creatures, newly awakened by the call of darkness. They left an invisible zigzag calligraphy in their wake. The bats were fast and erratic. I liked the bats the best.

BEN

Mom took me to the beach. Just me. N was at school. Sometimes being the little one wasn't half bad! It was a heavy day where the clouds hung so low and so engorged you just knew they were going to bust right open, but they didn't.

Mom and I walked together on the shoreline, holding hands. I liked the way the sand felt when it squished between my toes and the squeaky sound it made when my feet slid across it just right. We made a sand castle with a moat. We picked up shells and feathers and sang silly songs. When Mom sang to me, it was like a gift.

After our picnic lunch, Mom let me feed the Cheetos to the seagulls. They swarmed all around us—the greedy scavengers. I liked watching them catch the Cheetos in midair. I wondered if I would be able to do that when I got my wings. N could throw them to me, and I could swoop down and catch them in my mouth.

I sat there in the sand and looked at the waves, all dark and foamy that day, and I got awfully excited just imagining how once my wings came, I'd be able to fly out over the waves and see them from above.

I could fly clear across the ocean if I wanted, and go explore some other land. Maybe I'd find a place where everyone had beautiful reptilian wings. I knew there was a place like that somewhere—maybe an island or star or secret valley. And everyone there was waiting for me to get my wings and join them. Only thing was, Mom and Pop and N didn't have wings . . . so I wasn't sure how that would work out. I didn't know if I'd want to go without them.

I went with my mother and Ben to the doctor. Ben had to get a physical before he could start kindergarten. That's the law around here. I guess they don't want some kid with an infectious tropical disease getting all the other little tykes sick.

We went to see Dr. Abrams. My mother bribed us that if we were good she'd take us for milk shakes after Ben's appointment. I was sitting in the waiting room, just anticipating the taste of that milk shake. Strawberry was my favorite flavor. So there I sat, while Ben talked to my mother about his wings.

"What color do you think they'll be?" he asked her.

"Purple, with green stripes," said my mother in her teasing voice.

"No, Mama. Not purple. I think maybe greenish blue, like the ocean. What do you think about that?"

"Well, they'd match your eyes at least!" she said, touching the tip of her index finger to the end of Ben's nose.

"Mama, wings don't have to match," said Ben.

"Really . . . so you could have one orange one with yellow stripes, and one green one with red polka dots?"

"Mama! They have to match each other . . . I mean they don't have to match the rest of your body."

"Oh, I see."

"So what color do you think they will be?"

"Well . . ."

"*Benjamin Delaney,*" called the nurse standing in the doorway holding a clipboard.

"It's your turn, Ben. Come on, Ian," said my mother, taking my hand. The three of us followed the nurse through the door. Ben got weighed and measured; then we went into the examining room. After a while, in came Dr. Abrams.

"Well, Ben, you sure have gotten big!" she said. "And that can't be Ian so tall over there, can it?"

I liked Dr. Abrams. She was always cheerful, even if she did say predictable things. She looked in Ben's ears and flashed a light in his eyes and tested his reflexes and all of the usual stuff. Then Ben said, "Can you check for my wings?"

"Excuse me?" asked Dr. Abrams.

"Can you check for my wings?" By this point Ben had stripped off his shirt and turned his back to her. "My wings . . . are they ready yet?"

Dr. Abrams gave Mom a puzzled look.

My mother looked at Dr. Abrams and winked. "Ben thinks he's going to sprout some wings," she said.

"Well then, I better take a look," said Dr. Abrams. She began examining Ben's back. She made quite a production out of it, using various doctor tools and saying long, tangled words. Finally, she turned Ben toward her and said, "I don't think they are ready yet, Ben." She and my mother both chuckled a little.

I could tell Ben knew they were teasing, and it made him angry. He pulled his shirt over his head inside out, crossed his arms, and pouted.

Even the promise of a milk shake didn't placate Ben. He refused to have one. And they were out of strawberry so I had to settle for chocolate.

BEN

I'll never forget the day I discovered the stairway to heaven. It was right there in my closet. We lived in this ancient two-story farmhouse with a steep roof. N and I shared the bedroom at the top of the stairs, and Mom and Pop slept down the hall. Anyway, this room N and I slept in had a huge closet attached to it. We played in that closet a lot, especially on rainy days.

We made up a game called "The Bears are Sleeping." We'd make caves in the closet out of blankets and big empty cardboard cartons. The idea was that when we finished making the caves, we'd crawl into them and be hibernating grizzlies. I don't think we ever got to the point of actually doing the grizzly part of the game, but we sure made elaborate cave complexes.

On this one heavy, dark afternoon when I was five, we were in that closet making architecture when I saw a string hanging from the ceiling. How I'd never noticed that string before is a mystery to me. I mean, I was a kid who was always looking up.

"Hey, N, what's that?" I asked, pointing.

"I dunno," he answered as he lined a cave with an old, moth-eaten afghan.

"N, you have to look," I insisted.

"Okay, Ben, what?" He poked his head out of the box, and again I pointed to that dangling piece of string.

"That's string," said N, and went back to what he was doing.

"I know it's string, N, but what's it for?"

"Who knows!"

I pushed the biggest box we had so that it was positioned directly beneath the string. I climbed on top. I couldn't reach.

I piled another box onto the first. When I scrambled to the top again, the boxes collapsed and I tumbled across the closet floor.

"Hey, N, help me," I said, grabbing the rope handle of an old wooden trunk. We positioned it beneath the string. I stood on top, but I was too small to come close to my goal. I got the straight-back chair from the bedroom and placed it on the trunk. Then I retrieved the small wooden step stool from the bathroom, stacked it on the chair, and carefully scaled my makeshift ladder.

I was finally grasping that dirty old hank of string in my fist. I tugged. I knew something was supposed to happen, but nothing did. So I pulled again, and this time I lifted my feet. The string opened a magic door, and the stairway to heaven unfolded right there, scattering my wooden tower across the closet floor. I landed in a heap on a smashed cardboard carton.

"Whoa, N, look at that!" I said.

But N was already looking.

"Come on," I said, dashing up those magic stairs. I ran across the attic floor to the window where I looked out. I'd never been this high off the ground before. Those stairs had to be the key to some secret of flight.

N poked his head through the gaping mouth at the top of the stairs. "Ben, you better come out of there," he called. "Mama didn't say you could go up there."

But I wasn't budging.

Course, N told me those stairs weren't really magic. They were just folding attic stairs that lots of houses have. But to me, they expanded the universe. The attic became my private lair. I brought my treasures up there. I pulled a battered table from a jumble of other discarded furniture and dragged it across the floorboards to the window. I found an embroidered tablecloth in a trunk of old linens and covered the table with it. I didn't care if the cloth had some holes. It was nice to see the warmth of the wooden tabletop winking through. I spread my things out there, and made a sort of shrine.

I had birds' eggs and pretty rocks and bleached animal bones. I had dried-out, hollow bodies of dead insects. Abandoned wasps' and hornets' nests. Seashells and fish scales and pinecones. Twisted pieces of wood and broken shards of colored glass and china. And some chandelier crystals Aunt Anna once gave me that I hung in the window, where they cast glittering rainbows around my kingdom.

But the best thing I had was my feather collection. I had hundreds of feathers that I stored in cereal boxes.

Blue jay feathers, now, they're real pretty, but common. I filled two Rice Krispies boxes with blue jay feathers.

I kept my seagull feathers in four big Cheerios boxes. Every time we went to the beach I came home with a whole gob of seagull feathers. They must shed a lot or something. Course, I didn't categorize my seagull feathers according to specific species or anything scientific. I was only five! I considered any feather I found at the beach a seagull feather, even though there were certainly some pelican, tern, and osprey feathers mixed in.

My best feathers—my rarest and prettiest—I stored in a Kellogg's Corn Flakes box. I had some quail and owl feathers Pop had found for me while inspecting trees for the paper company. I also had some bluebird feathers. They were bright ultramarine blue. I got them from Mr. Rayfield, who lived near us and had lots of birdhouses. My favorite was an ostrich plume. It barely fit in the box. N got it for me when his class went on a field trip to an ostrich farm. It was soft and wispy, and would have been perfect for the hat of a pirate or a musketeer.

So that's how I discovered the stairway to heaven and established my attic kingdom, my elevated realm.

IAN

When Ben was in kindergarten, my mother went to the annual kindergarten conference, where the parents got to hear the teacher tell whether or not their child was socially and academically well adjusted. That night, after dinner, my mother and father were sitting at the table talking. My mother was telling my father about the conference. They didn't know I was just on the other side of the door, listening. I did a lot of that back then, listening.

"Ben is very popular with the other kids. Mrs. Landry called him magnetic."

"Takes after his amazing father!"

My mother ignored his remark. "And Mrs. Landry said that Ben is a wonderful student. Very quiet and cooperative. And smart as a whip."

"Well, I'm not surprised. We've never had any complaints about Ian, and it stands to reason that Ben would follow suit," said my father. (I puffed up proudly when he said that bit about me.)

My mother sighed. "Well, dear, you missed the point.

Mrs. Landry said Ben's wonderful *in the classroom*. On the playground, it's an entirely different thing."

"What do you mean?" asked my father.

"Well, you know how Ben is with all of his flying business. It's the same way at school. Mrs. Landry said that he's reckless and dangerous on the playground . . . jumping and diving and flapping with no regard whatsoever to how high off the ground he is or who might be in his way. And apparently the other children like to imitate him, because he has *leadership qualities*." (I'm ashamed to admit it now, but at the time, I was delighted to hear that my little brother was not the model citizen that I was. It was that nasty beast called sibling rivalry rearing its ugly head.)

"So he's a little wild? He's a kid."

"It's more than a little wild, I think. Mrs. Landry used the phrase *out of control*."

"Ben's always had a lot of energy."

"It's his recklessness that concerns her," explained my mother.

"He is somewhat reckless," admitted my father.

"And she said he's always talking about flying."

"Where did this flying thing of Ben's come from anyway?" asked my father.

"I wish I knew. I can't remember a time when that boy wasn't trying to fly."

BEN

Pop taught me a new word. Who would have believed such a word existed! *Gravity.* I liked the way it sounded. It kind of rolled off my tongue like a wave breaking on the sand. Think about it . . . *Gravity* . . . *Gravity* . . . *Gravity* . . . you could be sitting on the beach, and the ocean could be calling that word out to you, day and night, forever.

I thought it was good that I learned my enemy's name. Gravity. See, when you don't know your enemy's name, the threat seems blacker.

And Pop told me that Gravity was what made you go down instead of up. So it's understandable that Gravity became my enemy, right?

Ben was always so daring. I could never have done half the stuff he did. One of his favorite tricks was to climb through the attic window and crawl out onto the roof. And, being Ben, he didn't simply sit in the middle of the roof—no, he sat right on the edge—even dangled his legs over the side sometimes. And he wasn't scared the tiniest bit. Naturally, our parents didn't know that Ben went out there. He swore me to secrecy.

Ben's favorite time to go on the roof was when the stars were out. At night, he tried to stay awake until our mother and father went to bed. Then he climbed his stairway to heaven and went through the window. Sometimes I could hear him singing on the shingles.

I went with him once. The stars looked beautiful. But when I looked at the ground below, it made my legs feel like rubber bands. I was almost too frightened to crawl back to the window, because that meant I had to get real close to the edge. Ben called me a ground-dweller.

BEN

N always liked to play with little Hot Wheels cars, or plastic army men, or LEGO blocks. I liked to play with mummies. Sounds pretty weird, but they weren't actually mummies. We just called them that. They were the dried-out shells of dead insects. Easy to find if you knew where to look. One of the best places was between the screens and the windows. They seemed to get trapped there, so they died. Then their bodies dried out. Like mummies. Mainly we'd find common ones—houseflies, mayflies, and roaches. Those weren't very powerful. They'd be pawns in a game of chess. Dragonflies and wasps, however, were pretty powerful. And yellow jackets—now, they were megapowerful. So were hornets.

Sometimes my insects would fight N's plastic army men. His guys had guns and tanks and stuff, but my mummies had venom and stingers and fangs. Besides, we played in my kingdom, so I had an edge anyway.

Usually N was a pretty calm general, but during one war he got mad at me and smashed most of my mummies.

I couldn't believe he did that. Littered on the floor of my kingdom were flakes of petrified insect, their wings shattered, their heads and abdomens and thoraxes crushed. I didn't let N back in my kingdom for days after that. Not till he found me two dragonflies and three yellow jackets.

This happened when Ben was still Ben. In other words, before Ben was Icarus. I think he was six, maybe seven, so I'd have been eight or nine.

It was autumn. There was a refreshing coolness in the air. The sky was bright blue and cloudless. One day after school, my father was going to practice passing and dribbling with me, so I ran upstairs to get the soccer ball.

Ben was in our room, sitting cross-legged on his sheet, which he had carefully spread flat on the floor. In his lap was a tangled gnarl of clothesline, rope, and string. I recognized that gnarl. It was usually in an old laundry basket in the barn. It had been around for as long as I could remember. My father always said, "That mess is too good to throw out, but too much trouble to untangle."

"What are you doing?" I asked Ben.

"Making something," he replied, not looking up.

"What?"

He cheered as he extracted a length of clothesline from

the mess in his lap. He tied one end of the clothesline to one corner of the sheet.

"Ben, what are you making?"

"You'll see."

"Tell me."

But he was absorbed in his detangling efforts and didn't reply. I shrugged, rolling my soccer ball out from under my bed and down the stairs. I was used to Ben getting so sucked into his ideas and schemes that he didn't respond to outside stimulus.

My father was waiting for me in the yard. "Is Ben coming?"

"No, he's busy."

"Doing what?"

"Dunno. Making something."

My father and I kicked around the soccer ball for a while. When we got tired, we sat together on the swing hanging from the live oak tree in the yard. My mother came to sit with us. She brought my father a beer and me an orange Popsicle. I felt great. I had my parents all to myself. I had a Popsicle. It was Friday, so there was no school the next day. Life was perfect!

What happened next was both instant and eternal. It was a time curve kind of thing.

"Hey, everybody, watch this!" I looked toward the sound of Ben's voice. Which meant I looked up. So did my mother and father. There, on the edge of the roof, a good twenty-five feet above the ground, balanced Ben. Right on the edge. He looked awfully tiny up there. My father jumped to his feet and dropped his beer. My mother screamed. I watched, frozen.

And Ben? Ben jumped. I saw a field of white billowing behind him in an oblong blob. Suddenly I knew what Ben had been doing upstairs with that sheet and that ball of collected twines and ropes.

I grabbed my mother by the wrist. "It's okay, Mom, Ben's got a parachute."

And Ben fell like a streak and fell some more and no one breathed at all and time stood still. I couldn't figure out why the parachute didn't open. We had those toy army men with parachutes, and they worked pretty well. But Ben's parachute didn't work at all. As he fell, my mother and father ran across the yard toward the potential point of impact.

And while I do not believe in God every minute of every day, I know he was there then because I saw a branch of that live oak tree reach out and grab Ben's parachute, or sheet, depending on your perspective. So there was Ben, shirtless, suspended about ten feet from the ground, his parachute cords laced through the belt loops of his jeans.

"That was great!" said Ben, smiling. He made an art form of saying the wrong thing at the wrong time. My mother and father did not find anything great about seeing their son dangling from the tenuous branch that had just saved his life.

"Get him down, Frank," my mother cried out, her face chalky and her voice quavering. "Hurry." She was standing directly beneath Ben, reaching for his bare feet, but they were way over her head. "Benjamin, are you hurt, honey?" she called up to my brother.

"No, Mama. Not hurt at all. I almost flew, Mama!"

"Benjamin Delaney, you cannot fly. You cannot fly! *You cannot fly.*" She was coming unglued. I sat back on the swing—sucking on my Popsicle and wishing I had half the nerve Ben had.

My father returned from the barn with the ladder and managed to bring Ben back to earth, physically at least.

Ben knew he was in big trouble. Once they had finished hugging and kissing him and checking for injuries, my parents lit into him like a nest of angry hornets. He had an endless list of chores to do that weekend and couldn't leave the house at all, not even to sit on the porch. For Ben, that was heavy-duty punishment. He hated to be cooped up inside.

BEN

I had believed that my parachute would work. It was designed after one of those paratrooper army man toys, with a rope in each corner. They shouldn't make toys that lie to children.

After my failure, I went to the public library, where Mom worked, and got a book about parachutes, and real parachutes weren't designed at all like the ones on those useless toys. Oh, they had lots of different parachute designs, believe me, but none like that. Someone ought to make them stop producing those false playthings.

Still, free-falling had been great. Almost like flying. I had hoped my wings would suddenly emerge. That's why I'd taken off my shirt—so my wings would open right away. If they had, it sure would've made my life easier. See, once my wings came, I'd fly away to find other people like me, and learn all of the secrets they possess.

That night—the night of my failure—I told N that it was worth it. I didn't care if I did have to do all of those chores and stuff. There's always a price, isn't there? That's what I said. I meant what I said.

But then, while I was in my first-grade classroom a few days later, putting my spelling words in alphabetical order (*bad, bed, bid, bud,* etc.), anticipating lunch and recess, sabotage was taking place at home.

School seemed pretty good that day. I even found a real treasure on the playground—the wing feather of a male cardinal, all scarlet and bold. The minute I got home I raced up the stairs and into my closet. I reached for the string. It wasn't there. I flipped on the light. My breath caught in my throat. The trapdoor, the golden gate to my kingdom, was nailed shut. I mean seriously, permanently nailed shut. There were one-by-four planks blocking entry into my hallowed place. I sank to the floor and looked down at the bright splash of a feather in my hand. My treasures . . . they were all up there.

I felt cheated. I felt almost as cheated as I had the day I was born, when I realized there were no wings on my back; when I thrashed like a fly caught in a web.

I was angry, vexed, ferocious. I kicked my closet walls. I screamed and shrieked. I would have cussed, but at that time in my life I didn't know any cusswords. I kicked my closet walls like a percussionist gone mad. I clawed at the things on my closet shelves and dashed them to the floor, only to further abuse them by stomping on them. Worst of all, I cried. Big old tears the size of marbles rolled down my face and into my mouth. That made me even madder because I wasn't some crybaby kind of kid. Usually I was tough as nails—at least when it came to physical pain. But this . . . this was personal. My kingdom had been breached.

IAN

After Ben tried to parachute off the roof, I overheard my mother and father having one of their private conversations. I was crouched, silent and invisible, in the living room corner behind my mother's ficus tree. My parents were sitting on the sofa in the dark, so the only light was whatever spilled through the hallway door.

"I don't get it, Frank. Ben is so smart. Why would he do such a thing?" She took a sip of her wine.

"He's a kid, Olivia. He thought it would work."

"But Frank, any six-year-old has enough judgment not to attempt such a stunt." She paused. "It's a miracle . . . he could have . . ." I heard her voice break with a sob. My father put his arm around her.

"It is a miracle. You're right. When I saw him falling . . . I thought . . . I feared . . ." My father stopped speaking. His voice trembled with the weight of the words he was afraid to utter.

My mother sniffled and wiped her eyes. "Frank, how do we keep him safe? What do we do?"

My father took her hands in his. "I wish I knew, Olivia. I wish I knew."

"It's been one crazy stunt after another ever since he could crawl. It's only going to get worse as he gets older and stronger."

"Maybe. But we can't tie him to a chair."

"But Frank . . ." She was sobbing again.

"What about a doctor—" my father began.

"Ben is not crazy, Frank. I'm not sending him to some shrink who will convince him that he was Superman in a past life or something equally ridiculous. We've talked about this before, and you know how I feel."

"All right, Olivia. No doctor. I just thought after what happened you might have changed your mind. I love Ben with all my heart, but we have to face it . . . our son believes he has wings. I think they call that delusional."

My mother glared daggers at my father. She got up and paced back and forth on the rug in front of the sofa. "Enough, Frank," she snapped. "Ben's just imaginative . . . creative."

"Olivia, he doesn't know the difference between fantasy and reality. It's dangerous. *He's* dangerous."

"Please don't say those things. He's my baby. . . ." Her sobs again broke her speech.

My father sighed and ran his hand through his hair. "He's my baby, too, Olivia. Don't forget that. He's my baby, too."

"I know, Frank. I know." My mother sat beside him and put her arms around his neck.

I thought this was a good time to make an escape. I slipped soundlessly from my hideaway.

BEN

I never knew that I could be hurt so badly, wounded so deeply. Why, why had those who loved me taken from me what I treasured most?

The closet floor became my grieving place. Every day after school that week, I mourned there, gazing at the obstructed gates to my kingdom. N would stand in the doorway, entreating me to come out. I could barely see him through the fire of my rage.

One evening, Pop came in when I was fuming on the closet floor. He stood over me. "Ben, come to dinner," he said.

I turned my back to him.

"Ben, I said to come to dinner."

I drew my knees to my chest and tucked my face in the cavity between my knees and torso so that I couldn't see his eyes and he couldn't see mine.

"Benjamin. Please get up now." His voice was flat and heavy.

I didn't move. Didn't even breathe. I thought if I was still and quiet enough I might become invisible.

He grasped me beneath my armpits and pulled me from the floor. I did not unfold my body.

"Please, Ben," he said, a sharp edge creeping into his voice. I remained rigid.

Pop sighed. "Fine. Stay here and pout. Don't eat your dinner." He dropped me back on the closet floor and slammed the door as he left. I knew he was really angry. Pop never slammed doors. I sat alone in the darkness.

I think I fell asleep. Or just drifted, maybe. I heard the doorknob squeak, and light fell across my face as the door cracked open.

"Hey, Ben," said Pop softly. He sat down on the floor beside me and stroked my hair. It felt nice. Neither of us said anything for a while.

Finally I asked, very quietly, "Papa, did you do it?"

He sighed. "Yes, Ben, I did."

"Why, Papa, why?" I was trying not to cry, but I could hear my voice trembling. I took a deep breath and closed my eyes.

"Ben, what you did last week—jumping off the roof— that was dangerous and reckless. You could have died, or been crippled for life." Pop pulled me onto his lap as he spoke. He wrapped his arms around me, the thumb of his left hand stroking my cheek. "I'm your father. I have to do whatever I can to keep you safe. Every time I think about how I felt when I saw you falling, I become physically sick. My stomach churns. My skin tightens. My muscles go slack."

"But, Papa, that was my special place." I had to stop talking or the tears, the betrayers, would slip from my eyes. I felt them there, awaiting their curtain call.

Pop hugged me tight. His arms felt strong and secure

around me. "Ben, I have to do what I can to keep you safe. Don't you see that?"

Those old tears did their dirty work and came stampeding down my face. I was sobbing now, big noisy gulps. "Oh, Ben," said Pop. "I love you so, so much." I buried my face in his chest. I could smell on him the sweetness of the outdoors.

Ben was obsessing again. This time it was about Gravity, his sworn enemy. He kept asking us what color Gravity was, as if we knew. My father said, "No color," and went back to reading the newspaper. My mother once more tried to explain Gravity in scientific terms, which Ben never adhered to. I evaded the whole issue by pretending I didn't understand Gravity at all.

Then one night at dinner, Ben put down his fork, folded his hands, and cleared his throat. "I think I have the answer," he declared. We all waited, not entirely sure as to the nature of the pronouncement. "Gravity's not pink or yellow. That's pretty obvious. Because Gravity's a heavy color. I thought about all the colors I know, and I think Gravity must be dark green, almost black, with streaks of crimson running through him. Gravity's male, too, just like sunlight is female." He smiled proudly as if he had just solved all the mysteries of the universe.

BEN

I got in trouble at school, which meant I got in trouble at home.

We were at recess. I was playing all by myself on the playground, not bothering a living soul. I was pretending my favorite big old moss-draped oak tree was a castle and I was a dragon trying to get in and save the princess from the evil sorcerer. So there I was, having a grand time, circling that castle, when that tree called out to me and told me to climb him. He was a great climbing tree, with branches leading here and there and to the sky and everywhere. In my fantasy, the princess was at the end of this thick branch that was about ten feet high, and pretty much parallel to the ground. I was shinnying my way out to save the princess when I heard Nathan Bently call out, "Ms. Rivera, Ben Delaney's up in the tree."

Ms. Rivera and about a million second graders came running over. Some of the kids were laughing, and some of them were cheering, and some of them were saying, "Ms. Rivera, Ben Delaney's up in the tree," as if she couldn't see that with her own two eyes.

Ms. Rivera looked up at me, and I looked down at her. "Benjamin Delaney, you get out of that tree this minute," she hollered.

"Yes, ma'am," I said. I threw my left leg over the branch I was straddling; then I jumped right out of that tree, landing on both feet smack in front of Ms. Rivera.

"Are you hurt, Ben?" she asked in a panicky voice.

"No, ma'am."

"Are you sure?" She was checking my legs, like she thought they might be broken.

"My papa says my bones are made of rubber," I said proudly.

"Don't get smart with me, Ben Delaney." Then she yelled, "Everyone get in line, *now*, and I want absolute silence."

So all the kids scurried into line, and James Chavers said to me, "Great, Delaney, we have to go back to class all 'cause of you," and he jabbed me in the ribs with his elbow.

We filed into the building. Ms. Rivera stopped us in the hallway by the main office. "Not a word," she cautioned, and she asked the office lady for paper and a pen and started writing something. Then she said, "Benjamin, this is for Mrs. Halen. You are to go talk with her."

"Yes, ma'am," I said, taking the folded paper. I couldn't believe she was sending me to the principal's office. I felt the paper in my hand, a missive of certain disaster. I walked into the main office. The office lady was on the phone. I slipped quietly into a chair next to the wall.

Then the office lady hung up and said, "What can I do for you?" like I was an important customer at the bank or something.

"I'm supposed to see Mrs. Halen."

"Indeed! And what is your name?"

"Ben Delaney."

"Oh, you must be Ian's brother. He's such an angel. So

38

polite and respectful." (People always said stuff like that about N.)

"Yes, ma'am. He's in fourth grade."

"Well, Ben Delaney, by the look of you, I don't think you were sent here for a serving of praise. Let's go. Come on . . . this way." I followed her down a short hallway to Mrs. Halen's office, otherwise known as the Death Chamber. I'd been there before . . . a few times.

Even though I never told anyone, not even N, I always thought Mrs. Halen was kind of pretty. She had these lovely dark brown eyes with thick eyelashes. Mrs. Halen was sitting at her desk writing. She looked up when the office lady said, "Excuse me, Mrs. Halen."

"Ben Delaney, right? Second grade?" said Mrs. Halen.

"Yes, ma'am." Those dark eyes looked right inside mine.

"Ben, we've got to stop meeting like this," she said, and she and the office lady laughed. Then Mrs. Halen told the office lady, "Thank you. I'll see what I can do with him. . . . Come sit down, Ben."

I knew where to sit. Like I said, I'd been there before.

"Well, Ben, what happened?"

I looked at my hands. "I climbed a tree at recess."

"Ben, look at me when you talk to me. And speak up."

"I climbed a tree at recess." This time I looked right into her liquid brown eyes.

"Now, Ben, you've been sent here before for climbing trees . . . last year, remember?"

"Yes, ma'am."

"And we talked about it then, didn't we?"

"Yes, ma'am."

"And you said you'd never do it again."

"I forgot."

"Why do you think we don't let our students climb trees?"

39

"That's something I never could figure out, Mrs. Halen. Seems like a waste of those great climbing trees to me."

Mrs. Halen got a funny look on her face. I didn't know if it was good-funny or bad-funny. "Ben, what if someone fell out of a tree and got hurt?"

"Who'd fall out of a tree?" I asked.

"Not everyone can climb as well as you can, Ben. What if another child saw you, and copied you, and got hurt?"

"But I was playing by myself," I explained.

"That's not the point, Ben. Our rule against tree climbing addresses basic safety issues. Like the rule against running in the hall."

"I never could figure that one out either," I told her, and she looked exasperated.

"Ben, you don't have to like the rules, you just have to observe them. Okay?"

"Yes, ma'am," I said. "Oh—I forgot to give you this." I reached out to hand her Ms. Rivera's note. Mrs. Halen unfolded the paper and read it. I watched her shiny dark eyes, and they gave nothing away.

Finally she put the note down and looked at me. "What else did you do, Ben?"

"What else?"

"Ms. Rivera wrote about something else."

"I don't remember what else," I said, wondering if I had been disrespectful.

"Ms. Rivera says in this note that you jumped out of the tree."

"Yes, ma'am. I did."

"Why?"

"Ms. Rivera said get down, and that's what I did."

"Ben, you had to know that she didn't mean for you to jump."

"She said right now," I protested.

"Ben." Those pretty eyes were reading me.

"I won't do it again, Mrs. Halen. I promise."

"I'm going to have to call your mother, Ben."

"Today?"

"Yes, Ben. Today."

"But she's at work. We aren't allowed to call her at the library."

"Well, I am, and I have that number."

"Yes, ma'am." I decided maybe she didn't have such fantastic eyes after all.

So naturally, Mom and Pop got mad at me, too. They battered me with that word again . . . *reckless*. It was like standing in a rainstorm, and the raindrops were that word, pelting me from all sides—*reckless, reckless, reckless*. . . .

Mom made me write Ms. Rivera and Mrs. Halen letters to apologize for the trouble I caused. Then she made me rewrite the letters because she said the first ones were too sloppy. And Pop made me sweep the front porch and rake the yard. At least he gave me outdoor jobs. It was the inside ones I really hated.

Ben woke me up. He was screaming and thrashing around like a fish on the beach. I got out of my bed and went to his, where I pushed at his shoulders to wake him up. He was all sweaty lying there, and out of breath. When he opened his eyes and saw me, he clung to me.

"I think I had a nightmare, N," he said. "It was horrible. Gravity was hiding under the porch steps and every time I tried to get inside the house he grabbed my ankles. Did you know Gravity can change shape? He can. This time he was like an octopus, reaching out with all those tentacles, trying to wrap them around my ankles so he could drag me under the house and devour me.

"I thought I could trick him. Instead of walking up the steps, I was gonna climb over the porch rail on the side of the house. I was halfway over the rail when he got me. I grasped the rails as hard as I could, but N, Gravity's awful strong, and I was losing my grip. I was calling for help, for Papa or Mama or you, but nobody came, and one of my hands let go of the rail and then another tentacle came and coiled around my wrist and my other hand slipped. I couldn't even breathe." He held on to me tight. "I'm so glad you saved me, N. Gravity was awful hungry, there under the house."

The rest of the night, I slept in Ben's bed with him. And Ben, who had never been afraid of anything that I could remember, became terrified of the space under the porch. He would get a running start when he was entering or leaving the house, so that he could jump over the steps and not have to touch them. He was absolutely certain that Gravity was lurking there, waiting for him, hungry and vicious.

BEN

It was the dullest, most boring, colorless, textureless, uninteresting, unstimulating, mundane week of the whole school year. In other words, sharpen your number-two pencils and turn off any ounce of creative energy running around in your blood. The week of the dreaded standardized tests, where you are measured against all the other kids in the state or nation or world or whatever, and some document is sent out a few months later, telling you, by percentages, whether you are stupid or smart when compared to all of the other victims. So like, if you're smart, you're smart enough to know it without taking the test, and if you're not smart, believe me, someone, somewhere makes sure you know it, so what's the point?

Anyway, they tell you to eat a good breakfast and get a lot of sleep and all that stuff, and you get to school and the teacher says to clear your desk, then goes into some lengthy explanation of what that means. She passes out the test booklet, which says in big letters on the front cover and on every page: DO NOT MAKE A MARK IN THIS TEST

BOOKLET. But just in case you're too stupid to see those messages graffitied all over the place, your teacher says it, too.

So there I was, sitting in my seat near the window, and Mrs. Chandler, my fourth-grade teacher (who I called Mrs. Hitler because she was mean as a hyena), said to us, "Keep your eyes on your own paper (Like who cheats on those bubble-in-the-answer tests?). No talking. Do not make any marks in the test booklet. Do not work ahead. If you finish a section before the time is up, check your work, or rest your head on your desk." Then we spent about a year filling in the bubbles on the answer sheet so the machines would know our names and stuff.

It was finally time to get started. Mrs. Hitler read the little speech telling us what we were being tested on (reading vocabulary was the first one) and how much time we had. Then she said, "Pencils up . . . go!" Oh, brother. So I filled in all the little bubbles to let the machine know that I knew my vocabulary words. There was still time left over. Now, be honest, even though they tell you to, do you ever go back and check your work? I don't think real people do that.

Anyhow, I got to thinking, wondering what would happen if I did make a mark in that test booklet. So right there next to the big bold letters that said DO NOT MAKE A MARK IN THIS TEST BOOKLET, I drew a picture of N—a cartoon where he had buckteeth and scrappy hair. And guess what? Nothing happened. The sky didn't fall. The earth didn't quake. The oceans didn't swallow us all up with a big burp. Nothing.

Then, even though at the bottom of the page it said, STOP. DO NOT GO ON TO THE NEXT PAGE, I turned the page in my test booklet. And nothing happened there, either. No bells or whistles. No sirens in the distance. Nothing.

Finally Mrs. Hitler said, "Pencils down. Close your test booklets," and I heard all those number-two pencils hitting the desks, and all this paper rattling, and kids were sighing like they'd just accomplished something really big. Then Mrs. Hitler said, "I'll give you a five-minute break to stretch." You'd have thought she'd given out Christmas presents or something the way some of those kids were acting.

By the end of the day, I had a headache. I really hated those stupid tests. I hated filling in those dots all day. So I walked home from the bus stop, dreading the rest of the week because I knew it was going to be more of the same.

When I entered the house, Mom called me. She was in the kitchen, holding a book and a shoe box with holes punched in the top. "Ben, I found something. Something you'll like. Come here." I went to stand next to her at the table and she handed me the shoe box. "Open it," she said.

I lifted the lid and couldn't believe what I saw. In that shoe box was a moth. A huge, beautiful one. "Mama, thanks," I said in awe. "You're the best."

That moth had to have been magic. Nothing could be that pretty without having some magic stirred in some-where. It was big; bigger than my hand. It had what looked like eyes, one on every wing. The top wings had dark red bor-ders across the upper edges, and the bottom wings had long curved swallow-tailed kind of things, all graceful and lovely. The antennas looked like tiny brown feathers. The wings were green; soft pale green, like a mystery at night. I sat there looking at that beautiful moth, not saying any words because there weren't any words. Sometimes your eyes and heart do the talking.

Mom waited a long time, just letting me look. Then she opened the book, called *Butterflies and Moths,* to the page she had marked. "Look," she said. I read the caption beneath the picture. Luna moth; *Actias luna.* I read all about the luna moth. It lives in North America, from Canada through the United States and all the way to Mexico. When it's a caterpil-

lar, it eats like crazy, gobbling up leaves. Then it makes its cocoon, and after a while it hatches. But the sad thing is this:
that magical, beautiful moth lives for only about one week.
Only one week. And it doesn't even have a mouth. It can't
eat a thing. Or reveal any secrets. Or sing. Its only job is to
reproduce.

I looked at that beautiful moth for a while longer.
"Mama, would you be mad if I let it go?"

"No, Ben, I was hoping that's what you would do."

See, if it only gets to live for one week, it shouldn't have to
live in a shoe box. Not for even any extra minutes. I took the
box outside, but the moth didn't fly away, even when I used a
twig to push on its legs.

"It's sleeping," said Mom. "Remember, it's nocturnal,
which means it sleeps during the day."

I stuck my finger under its feet, since you're not supposed to touch the wings, and lifted it out of the box. It felt
funny, sort of ticklish, where it clung to my finger. Then I put
the luna moth on the porch rail. I sat there all afternoon
watching that moth, waiting for it to fly. Guess that's how N
felt, waiting for my wings to emerge, so he could see me fly.

BEN

Mrs. Hitler sent me to the principal's office. She got mad at me because I called her a ground-dweller. She said I was being disrespectful. But she was a ground-dweller. And if I had wanted to, I could have thought of worse things to call her.

She told us to write a paper about what we were going to do when we grew up, so naturally, I wrote about my destiny—about how great it would feel to fly, soaring over the world with my wings spread wide, everything looking little and tidy from way up there. I described the sense of freedom that would rush through me, that feeling I've been seeking all my life. Mainly, though, I explained how once I got my wings, I'd fly away to that secret place where other winged people live to learn all about their world, and the way they interact with this world of ground-dwellers. I thought my paper sounded pretty good when I turned it in.

Most of the kids wrote about being lawyers or race-car drivers or rock stars—stuff like that. All of which was fine with Mrs. Hitler, but she said my paper was unacceptable, and if I didn't want to get a big fat F, I would have to do it over again. So I told her, "You just don't understand 'cause you're a major ground-dweller."

That's when she totally lost it and sent me to Mrs. Halen's office. There I sat in my usual chair, with the principal's shiny brown eyes framed between long eyelashes looking at me.

"Ben, you know better than to call your teacher names," Mrs. Halen said after reading Mrs. Hitler's note. I didn't say anything. "What names did you call Mrs. Chandler?"

"I called her a ground-dweller," I muttered.

"A what?"

"A ground-dweller. She is a ground-dweller. So are you. So are my parents and my brother. I didn't mean anything bad by it. I was just stating a fact," I protested.

"Ben, why would you call Mrs. Chandler a ground-dweller?"

I tried to explain about writing the paper, and how one day I was going to fly, but I got everything tangled up, and Mrs. Halen looked confused.

"Ben, you need to take your assignments more seriously. Now, I want you to sit here and write another paper for Mrs. Chandler. This one needs to feature a real career—one where you would get paid. Do you understand?"

"Yes, ma'am," I said. I was really mad, but I tried not to show it. I had written a good paper about flying. I *had* taken that stupid assignment seriously. And now I had to do another one. So this time, I wrote about wanting to drive a street-sweeper when I grew up. I talked about how pretty the streets would look once I'd swept them, and how my street-sweeper would be the nicest one in the entire fleet. I'd wash and wax it all the time. I'd keep its engine in tip-top shape. I'd change the oil regularly. All of the neighborhoods in the entire county would be requesting me as their official street-sweeper. Before too long, they'd be making street-sweeper cards, just like they make baseball cards, and the card with my picture on it would be the most valuable of all. I'd be the most famous street-sweeper driver on earth.

When I finished, Mrs. Halen read my essay. "Ben, I don't know what to think about you sometimes," she said in a wistful voice. "Go back to class and turn this in to Mrs. Chandler."

"Yes, ma'am."

So I went to my classroom. I'd missed lunch and recess, and Jeremy and Alex were laughing at me. Mrs. Hitler read my paper. She said, "Ben, this isn't a whole lot better," and Jeremy and Alex laughed at me some more.

TEN

Ben collected birds' nests. He lined them up in rows on the bookcase next to his bed after stashing his books in cardboard boxes.

Sometimes, when we were bored and just hanging around, he'd pick up a nest and check out all the different materials some now-homeless bird had used to weave it.

"Look, N. There's a piece of pink ribbon, right there."

"Great."

"And a sliver of tattered audiocassette. Amazing, isn't it?"

"Amazing." I turned a page in the magazine I was reading.

"And a strip of newspaper. Look, N."

"Ben, don't you ever feel guilty imagining some poor tired bird getting home at the end of a grueling day, only to find his nest missing? Stolen by a greedy collector out scouring the countryside for the dwellings of harmless little birdies. Don't you? It's somehow immoral, isn't it? To steal their homes?"

"N, I only collect abandoned nests."

"How do you know they're abandoned? How do you know the bird didn't just fly out for a quick snack, or go to visit his dear old granny bird, or whatever?"

When Ben was in fifth grade, he went through this stage of mirror writing. He wrote everything in reverse, so if you wanted to read his writing without getting a headache, you had to hold the paper up to a mirror. At the time, Ben was obsessed with Leonardo da Vinci, and that's how da Vinci wrote his diaries—in mirror writing.

It drove our mother crazy. She went to talk to Ben's teacher, Ms. Morgan, about it. She did not find a sympathetic ear there. Ms. Morgan was young and idealistic and talked about Ben's need for self-expression. Then she proudly withdrew a large, rectangular mirror from her desk drawer and said, "Just be prepared, like me," and smiled brightly.

"But you don't understand," our mother politely argued. "Ben has never conformed to anyone's standard if it interfered with his own. The more indulged he is, the further across the line he goes."

"Please, Mrs. Delaney, what line? There should be no lines! Ben is a highly intelligent, very creative child. To stifle that creativity could deprive the world of an Einstein, a

Mozart, a Rembrandt! You should do everything you can to nurture those special traits in Ben."

I wasn't actually there when my mother met with Ms. Morgan. This was another story I overheard. My mother and father were sitting on the porch one night, and I was lurking under the porch steps, my ears perked up like daisies in the morning.

In relating that episode to my father, my mother expressed her frustration with Ms. Morgan. "These teachers, with all of their crazy ideas, well—they aren't trying to raise a child like Ben. It's a miracle he's still alive! How many times have we taken him to the hospital? Well? I've lost track. And what other ten-year-old has had three concussions, even if two of them were minor? They were still concussions."

"Ben's not hurting anyone with his mirror writing," said my father softly.

"Not that, but look at all of the other things . . ."

I slipped out from under the steps and ran through the darkness to the barn. "Ben," I called out as I pushed the heavy door open.

"Over here," he said.

I walked up to the workbench where Ben was arranging some slender slats of wood.

"I'm framing 'em up," he said, referring to the wings he was trying to make. They had been designed by Leonardo da Vinci centuries ago. Ben had blown up the sketches he'd found in a library book and tacked them to the wall over the workbench. His plan was to stretch fabric onto the wooden frames and wear them. To fly. Now, understand, they never worked for da Vinci. Or anyone else. Ben—the eternal optimist.

"I've made a few modifications," he explained, pointing to the red pencil marks he'd made on the da Vinci sketches.

"You don't really think those things will allow you to fly, do you?" I asked him.

"Well, I'm tired of waiting for my real wings to emerge, so I gotta try something. Did you get the canvas?"

"It's under the house," I said. That's how I happened to find myself beneath the steps during my parents' conversation. I had been stashing some old sails I'd scavenged from Mr. Rayfield's junk pile. Not that I thought Ben would really be able to fly with those wings he was making, but he was so enthusiastic.

Every time Ben was up to one of his schemes, he counted on two things: my help, and the fact that our mother never went into the barn because she was terrified of rodents. (We often exaggerated the depth and breadth of the rat problem in the barn just for insurance against her!) If my mother had known the things Ben cooked up in that barn, she'd probably have burned the rickety old building down.

BEN

N didn't know a whole lot about birds. He thought I was some kind of criminal in the night, stealing nests from unsuspecting birds like a crazed thief going to a trailer park and hooking his truck up to someone's mobile home and just driving off with it.

Birds aren't like people. Birds only use their nests to lay their eggs in and raise their young. They don't live in nests year-round and watch TV and stuff. It's like seasonal housing. In the off-season, birds don't cozy up in their twig-and-twine houses and barbecue worms and drink martinis.

So to me, finding an old nest balanced in the branches of a tree or tucked up under the eaves was like finding a seashell at the beach. It only used to be someone's house.

BEN

I was eleven. It was almost the end of my fifth-grade year. I was restless. Something big was eating at me. Big and hungry. Gnawing at my soul when it thought I wasn't looking.

One night, I lay in bed gazing through the window at the sickle of a moon dangling from the sky. Suddenly, as if through divine inspiration, I was enlightened. I knew. It wasn't one of those gradual realizations where the pieces slowly come together. No. This was like a brain explosion. I knew. I knew just what that growling, teeth-baring, snarling hunger had been.

I looked at N's clock—1:38 in mean glowing red numbers. The house was as quiet as sorrow. I slipped out of bed, down the stairs, and outside to the barn. It was dark there, even with the heavy double doors both flung wide open, but I knew where to find what I needed. A crowbar, a claw hammer, a cat's-paw, and some wooden shims. The tools felt heavy and cold in my hands. They felt powerful. I carried them to my room, where N was wrapped in his dreams. I went to the closet, shut the door, and flicked on the light.

I looked up at the trapdoor: the barricaded gateway to my lost kingdom. After five years of exile, it was time for the Great Reclamation!

I surveyed the tools . . . not exactly a quiet collection of things. My mission relied upon stealth to ensure its success. The dead of night, with the oppressors sleeping just down the hall, was not the appropriate time for action. I hid the tools under a blanket on the closet shelf and crawled back into my bed with anticipation dancing in my blood.

In the morning, after everyone had left the house on various errands, I got the stepladder from the downstairs pantry and set it beneath the trapdoor. I stuck the hammer, cat's paw, and wooden shims in the pockets of my jeans, and held the crowbar like a scepter. Up on the ladder, I pried away the one-by-four planks restricting access to my domain. The planks splintered and split, and the nails wailed in protest, but my tools and my determination were strong. Ultimately, I reigned supreme. The gateway to my paradise was restored.

I pulled down my stairway to heaven.

Slowly, patiently, reverently, I reentered my kingdom. The light spilling through the window was soft and diffused. I saw my table, my shrine, in its place of honor near the window, but . . . something was wrong. I ran across the rough-hewn attic floorboards as a cry of dismay escaped my lips. My treasures were gone!

Gone were my seashells and bleached bones and birds' eggs. Gone were my twisted pieces of wood and abandoned wasps' nests. Gone were my magnolia cones and acorns. Gone were my cereal boxes of assorted feathers.

I turned to the window, to look for the ground-dwelling enemy below. Something glistened and flashed like fire on my skin. My chandelier crystals still hung there, casting prismatic magic around my lair. I fingered the glass rainbow-makers. Those—at least—they had missed. Those had stood guard during the years of banishment. Those had maintained my kingdom. And now, I was older, stronger, smarter. I would rebuild! Reoccupy! Reclaim! I would not be defeated.

BEN

I cherished my reclaimed attic kingdom. At first, I was careful to keep its rebirth a secret. N knew, but N would not betray me. He was loyal. Always. And it's not like anything bad went on up there anyway.

I was methodical in the reestablishment of my realm, carefully dividing the attic into two sections. The area near the window I claimed for my own, and in the darker half, I piled a heap of cast-off stuff.

I was still a collector, so I gathered my cereal boxes of assorted feathers, as well as my other treasures, and brought them upstairs. Some things I hung on the walls or from the ceiling. Other things I arranged on shelves I made from cement blocks and planks. I brought my special books up there, too, the ones about nature, including the *Butterflies and Moths* book Mom had given me, and the John James Audubon *Birds of America* book that N got for me at the del Toroses' yard sale. I put my notebooks and colored pencils in a cardboard box and took them to my private lair. I also brought things only I could see—my dreams, my secret wishes, my nightmares, my ambitions, my confusions, my fears. I slipped them into a dusty place so that I could sort them out later.

I discovered a cardboard carton labeled BEN in an old wardrobe. I opened it to find my lost treasures—the things that had been locked away so many years ago when my kingdom was invaded. I unpacked the box, and those items regained their places of honor among the newcomers.

I went to the barn and, one item at a time, I smuggled my creations—my kites, my gliders, my rocket ships—across the yard and up the stairs to paradise.

My Leonardo da Vinci wings, which never did work in spite of my modifications, I hung from the rafters. They floated above me like a magnificent moth. Geez, they were beautiful.

I had used thin slats of wood to make the frames. That part of the project took the longest. All the curves and angles had to be just right.

N got me some old sails out of Mr. Rayfield's junk pile. I stretched them across my frames and used Pop's staple gun to secure them in place. Then I trimmed off the excess fabric. They were so perfectly and tightly stretched that they pinged when I flicked them with my finger.

N got me some paint, too. He never did say from where. It was nice stuff, though, thin like watercolor, but permanent. When I painted my wings, that paint looked all soft and delicate, like light itself.

Then one Saturday, when Mom and Pop went to town, I tried them out. My wings, that is. First I tried to take off from the ground. I ran across the yard flapping like mad, but not even for one breath did I levitate.

"N, help me, would ya?" I asked my brother. He was my air traffic controller that day. "When I get to the loft, hand 'em up to me."

"Ben, don't be stupid. You'll get hurt."

"No I won't. They're gonna work. I just know it."

"Like all your other disasters?"

I didn't defend myself against that remark. "I think these wings are more like gliders. They need elevation to work," I explained.

"Right," said N skeptically.

"Just help me, would ya, N?"

N knew better than to argue with me. I'd worked too hard on those wings to just forget the whole endeavor. I climbed to the loft and N handed them up to me. I strapped them on. They felt nearly as natural as my regular skin. And they weren't heavy at all—not for the size of them. I ran the length of the loft till I was rocketing through the loft door, flapping away.

Then Gravity, my powerful enemy, grabbed me in his teeth and yanked me to the ground.

"You okay?" asked N, not knowing what to do because I was tangled in the splintered strut of my left wing.

"Yeah, I'm okay," I said, stumbling to stand while I surveyed the damage. "My wing broke."

"At least *you* didn't break," said N. "Can you fix it?"

"Yeah. I'll just splice these broken places." I fell into my thoughts, working out exactly what needed to be done. I unstrapped my wings and took them to the workbench. I started selecting wood to make my repairs.

N came to stand beside me. "Too bad they didn't work," he said.

"Yeah. I'm disappointed, but maybe it's wrong of me to use artificial wings just 'cause my real ones aren't ready yet. Kinda like rushing things, or cheating or something. Like an elusive sort of dishonesty. Bad karma. A jinx. Whadda you think, N?"

"Ben, I'm not so sure you have any real wings," he answered.

I really hated it when N said stuff like that. "N, I know what I know," I said emphatically.

"Right, Ben, but you could be wrong."

"N, I'm not wrong. Just wait, you'll see." I was cutting a wood slat with a razor knife. "Just wait."

"Ben, I've been waiting since you were born."

"Patience, N, patience."

I hung those beautiful wings from the rafters, and they became the guardian angel of my kingdom—the luna moth of my soul.

To Ben's surprise, our parents immediately discovered his return to the attic, but they didn't object. "I hope by now, at eleven years of age, you won't do anything as rash as parachute from the roof," my father said with a sigh.

"It's always nice to have a private lair, isn't it?" added my mother.

"Oh, yeah? Well, what about me, then? Can I have a private lair?" I asked.

"I don't see why not," replied my father.

"You could have the other half of the attic," suggested my mother.

"What! No, that's *my* place. He can't come there," protested Ben.

"There's plenty of room for both of you," said my mother.

Ben looked threatened. I guess he felt like he was on the verge of once again losing his kingdom.

"How about the barn loft?" suggested my father.

"Yeah, the loft," Ben eagerly chimed in. "It'd make a great hideaway for you."

"Maybe." I didn't want to commit myself.

"I'll help you set it up," urged Ben. "We can make it look great."

"Well, I guess the loft could be cool."

So Ben followed me to the barn, and we spent the next few afternoons fixing up *my* kingdom. Ben swept away the dust, and I dragged up some old chairs and a rickety card table. We stapled posters to the walls and ceiling and dangled wind chimes from the rafters. My father let me hang his hammock between two heavy columns. It looked pretty good, but once the work was done, I wasn't sure what to do. I read for a while. My pal Tony and I played dominos and checkers. I threw darts at magazine photos of the Cardinals pitcher who'd hit a triple in the bottom of the ninth, causing the Cubs to lose. By the end of the first week or two, I'd lost interest in the loft. I decided that I wasn't the sort of person who needed a lair or kingdom.

IAN

It happened the summer before I started eighth grade. I was getting ready to go out with some friends when Ben came into our room.

"I just loaded the wagon. Let's go," he said.

"Huh?"

"Well, we need to get some bait, but I packed the fishing rods and tackle, and the lantern. I made some sandwiches and put drinks in the cooler. Come on."

Suddenly I remembered that I'd promised to go fishing with Ben. "Sorry, Ben. I'm going to the movies. We can go fishing tomorrow night."

"We planned this yesterday."

"But I forgot, and I'm going out with Tony, Isabel, Nick, A.J., and Rebecca."

"You made plans with me." He crossed his arms and took a step toward me.

"But we can go fishing anytime." I buttoned my shirt.

"You always do this, N. You ditch me when your friends come calling. I'm sick of it."

"Ben, I'm not ditching you. We'll go fishing tomorrow."

"That's what you said yesterday, N. And the same thing happened last week. It happens all the time."

"I can't help it if things keep coming up."

"You don't have to go. You can say no. You can say, 'I told my brother we'd go fishing.' " He took another step toward me. "You make me sick."

"Ben, Isabel's going. You know I think she's hot."

He thrust his arms forward and pushed me against the chest of drawers. "You're a liar and a fake," he said.

Before I could respond, he was gone.

When I got home later that night, I noticed Ben wasn't in his bed. I gave it little thought, deciding he must be in his kingdom or in the barn. So I went to sleep, dreaming of Isabel, who'd let me hold her hand during the movie.

It wasn't until the next morning that I realized all of Ben's things were gone. His bookshelves were clear of his birds'-nest collection and his drawers were empty. When I looked under his bed, where he kept his books in cardboard boxes, there was nothing there. I opened our closet. The stairway to heaven was closed. I went downstairs. My parents were in the kitchen drinking coffee. "Where's Ben?"

"He left earlier. Said he was going exploring in the woods." Dad, whose degree was in forestry, loved it that Ben spent lots of time in the woods.

"Did he say when he was coming back?"

"No, but he packed a lunch." My mother gestured to the mess left behind on the counter where Ben had made sandwiches.

I hung around the house waiting for Ben, but he never showed up. Around five o'clock, I took off to the arcade with Nick. When I got home, I went up to Ben's kingdom. He was sitting in the window looking at the sky. He had set up an old sleeper-sofa beneath his Leonardo da Vinci wings, and I saw his birds' nests lined up on a shelf. "Hey, Ben."

He looked at me and said nothing.

"What're you doing?"

"I dunno. Just thinking."

"So you moved out?"

"Up. I moved up."

"We probably need our own spaces."

"Probably." He was gazing out the window. It was his way of building a wall between us.

"Ben, I'm sorry about yesterday. And the other times. I wouldn't like it if someone did that to me."

"It doesn't matter." His voice was offhand and distant.

"Ben, you're my brother, and probably my best friend, but I've gotta have other friends, too."

"That doesn't make it all right. We had plans. I don't do stuff like that to you."

"You don't get it, Ben. I love you and Mom and Pop, but it isn't enough. There are lots of people out there. It's a huge world."

"But N, you blew me off like I didn't exist. It's been happening all summer. I'm sick of it. Just leave me alone." He crawled through the window onto the roof. I didn't follow or call him back. It was like that most of that summer. Me on my turf, Ben on his. It could have been the Great Wall of China looming between us. Our mother even asked me what was going on, but I played dumb and acted like I didn't have a clue what she was talking about.

BEN

There was a cardboard box in the attic. Actually, the attic was full of boxes where people had put stuff no one used anymore, but the one that interested me was labeled SKETCHBOOKS. Mom had studied art in college. When N and I were little, she used to draw a lot, but after she started working at the library she didn't do much artwork.

I opened that box and looked through Mom's sketchbooks. Her black-and-white pencil drawings were beautiful—quiet and serene. Not like her paintings hanging downstairs or leaning against the walls of my kingdom. Those were wild things that begged, no, demanded attention. Color seemed to give her artwork its blood and breath.

All of her sketches were dated with tiny numbers penciled in the bottom right corner of the page. The subject matter covered a wide variety of images. Most were done in pencil, but a few were ink or watercolor or colored pencil.

It felt good to sit in the window of my kingdom with the sketches in my lap. Almost like Mom was sharing herself with me, even if she didn't know it. I picked up a sketchbook from when N was a baby. There were drawings of him sleeping, eating, playing, crying, sucking his thumb, everything.

Then there were portraits of me as an infant. In my crib, in Pop's arms, with N . . . and one I had never seen before. It was me, as a baby, with a beautiful set of dragon's wings wrapped around my body. This was among the rare drawings Mom had enhanced with colored pencil. The lines were delicate. I could see the texture of my wings, the stars in my eyes, the roses in my infant cheeks. A small smudged handprint, N's hand, obviously, dominated the bottom left corner. Had he been sitting with Mom while she drew that picture? Had she been making up a story for N, never dreaming the truth behind the fiction? I tore that drawing from the sketchbook.

When Mom came home from work, I ran down the stairs, drawing in hand. She saw me coming. "Ben, please help me with the groceries." I put the drawing on the table in the hallway.

As I was unpacking a bag full of produce, I heard N stampeding down the stairs. "What's for dinner? I'm starved . . . hey, Ben, look at this." He walked into the kitchen holding the drawing.

"It's mine." I took it from his hand.

"You drew it?"

"No." I looked at Mom standing at the counter putting things into the cabinet.

"She drew it?"

"Yeah."

"Mom, you drew this? Is it Ben?"

She turned. Her eyes fell onto the drawing. A tender smile crossed her face, but a hint of fear lurked there as well. "Years ago. When you two were just babies." She walked over to us and took the drawing. "I remember that day. You must have been about eight months old, Ben." She ruffled my hair. "We were spending the afternoon on the porch, and you kept rolling yourself up in your blanket . . . and Ian, this was your contribution. You wanted to see what I was doing, but your hands were dirty." She traced his small handprint with her index finger.

"But Mama, that's just how my wings are gonna look," I said.

"Ben, please. It's a drawing. Nothing more." She handed it back to N.

I took it from him. "Mama, it's more than that," I insisted. "You must have had some awareness of my destiny."

She sat in a chair. "Ben, please don't make this out to be more than it is. It's a drawing. Nothing more. You wrapped yourself in your blanket, and it reminded me of wings, so that's what I drew. That's all." There was finality in her voice, but in her eyes I could see something more. Denial. And fear.

I felt lonesome when I went back to my kingdom and hung that drawing on the wall.

BEN

I followed the stream of kids down the hall toward the lunch-room, wondering what I would do once I got there. No one I knew from elementary school was anywhere in sight. I saw N and some other eighth graders laughing and cutting up, but I knew he wouldn't like it if I joined him.

"Hey," said a dark-haired, dark-eyed boy as he fell into step beside me.

"Whassup?" I tried to sound cool and nonchalant.

"I sit behind you in class. Actually in two classes, math and science. It's that alphabetical order seating arrangement they like to do. My name's Mason Elliot. I'm after you on the list."

"I'm Ben Delaney . . . but everyone calls me Icarus."

"Icarus?"

"My middle name," I lied.

We sat at an empty table. "I went to St. Anthony's last year. No one from St. Anthony's goes here," said Mason. "This school is so much bigger, too."

"It's big, all right. Lots of people."

"And lots of classrooms. I got lost on my way to English!"

N walked up to our table, which surprised me. "So how's it goin'? You surviving?"

"Yeah."

"Have you done anything totally embarrassing yet?"

"No," I said, wondering if maybe I had but was just too clueless to know it.

I learned that Mason lived close enough that I could walk or ride my bike to his house. We started hanging out after school and on weekends. I liked having him for a friend, especially since N and I weren't spending much time together. So Mason and I did a lot of the things I used to do with N—fishing, building things in the barn, exploring in the woods, catching reptiles and amphibians. We did other things, too. More grown-up things like N had been doing for a couple of years already—going to the arcade, hanging out with girls at the park, roaming farther from home.

IAN

One morning after homeroom, a seventh grader named Maxwell came up to me. "Hey, Ian, I met your little brother. He's all right. He's probably the coolest sixth grader we have here. Course with a name like Icarus, he'd either have to be totally cool or an absolute loser."

"Icarus?"

"Yeah, Icarus Delaney. He said he was your brother."

"My brother's name is Ben," I said, but the wheels were clicking by now. "Isn't Icarus that kid from Greek mythology who tried to fly out of the labyrinth?"

"Yeah. That's why Icarus is such a cool name."

"And my brother said to call him that?"

"Yeah."

"My brother's a little strange, Max. Nice, but strange."

When I got home that day, I went to the bookshelf in the hallway. We have this mythology book that my father used to read to Ben and me when we were little. I hadn't looked at that book in years, but I knew it contained the story I was seeking. I could even visualize the illustration of a winged boy soaring toward the sun, the whole picture flooded with yellow. And now, in light of my brother's new identity, I thought a refresher course was in order.

I slipped the book from the shelf, and found the story of Daedalus and Icarus. Right away I noticed something that didn't surprise me: these pages were more ragged than any of the others. No doubt for months, maybe even years, Ben had pored over that story in bed.

I read about Daedalus and his son, Icarus. The two had been imprisoned by Minos in the Great Labyrinth and wanted to escape. Daedalus finally came up with an idea: they would make wings from the feathers of birds and fly to freedom. Father and son collected feathers and used them to make two sets of wings. The feathers were secured with wax. Daedalus and Icarus flew from the labyrinth, tasting freedom. But Icarus, unable to resist the promise of the sun, ignored his father's warning not to fly too high. Enticed by the sun's warmth and power, Icarus climbed higher and higher into the sky. He finally soared so close to the sun that its heat melted the wax binding his feathered wings, and poor Icarus tumbled from the sky and into the sea, his feathers catching the wind.

So my brother, in addition to all of his other delusions, had taken on a new identity—Icarus. Who reached too high, too far, too fast.

BEN

Mason and I always sat at the same lunch table. After a few weeks, other kids started joining us until a whole crowd gathered around every day.

A girl named Kaitlyn sat with us. She was petite with dark hair and green eyes. She would always pull her chair up next to mine. Sometimes she even had to squeeze in because someone else was already there. When she talked, she'd put her hand on my arm. People kept asking if she was my girlfriend. Then Mason said she told everyone she liked me. Kids acted like we were a couple, but we weren't. The whole thing embarrassed me. I tried to avoid her, but she always seemed to be right there.

Kaitlyn was in my social studies class. Mr. Fountaine required everyone to participate in History Fair. "Pick a partner, because teamwork is an important skill." I was kind of zoned out when he said that. Kids got out of their seats to sign the roster. Next thing I knew, Kaitlyn was standing at my desk. "I signed up to be your partner, Icarus."

"My partner?"

"For History Fair. We need to think of a topic. Mr. Fountaine wants our thesis statements by Monday. I'll call you."

I sat there, stunned. History Fair was a major event at our school. I remembered N spending hours and hours working with his partner on his project about the Iron Curtain. "Um . . . I wanna do an individual presentation."

"Weren't you listening? Sixth graders do team projects, seventh graders do individual, and eighth can do either. Don't worry. I'm a hard worker. Here, write down your phone number."

I know it was mean, but I wrote down Mason's number instead. She called me anyway. She thought I'd done it by accident. I didn't have the guts to correct her.

BEN

I got grounded . . . again. I always wished Mom and Pop would call it something else. *Grounded* is like profanity to a sky-bound person like me. Here's what happened. We kept getting wrong numbers on the telephone. Lots and lots of them. Course I didn't know who the wrong numbers were looking for because I never answered the phone when it happened. Then at dinner, Mom said to Pop, "Frank, I'm wondering if maybe we should get our telephone number changed. People keep calling here for someone named Icarus."

"Icarus?" My father looked puzzled.

"Yes, Icarus."

"Who's Icarus?"

"I don't know, but it's worrying me. I'm thinking maybe Icarus is the code name for some drug dealer or crime boss who gave out our telephone number by accident. It could be dangerous." (Did I mention that Mom can be the most paranoid person on earth sometimes?)

N looked at me and I looked at N and we both burst out laughing.

"What is so funny about that, boys?" Mom asked.

"I'm Icarus," I said proudly.

"*What?*"

"I'm Icarus. That's what everyone calls me now," I explained, laughing a little.

"Well, if you are Icarus, young man, then you are grounded." See, Mom's really loving and gentle and all of the motherly stuff, but she doesn't always share my way of thinking, and since she named me Benjamin, she was all insulted that I wanted to be called Icarus (which she called pagan!).

IAN

Tara called me on the phone. I could hear her friends giggling in the background. She talked about school and stuff like that. Then she asked me what I thought of Allie. I was evasive. So she said Allie liked me, which was good because Allie was really pretty and nice, but still, I wasn't sure what to say. Then Tara said, "Hang on."

Next thing I knew, someone was saying, "Hi, Ian."

"Hi." I wasn't sure who I was talking to.

"What're you doing?"

"Nothing really . . . Allie?"

"Well, who did you think it was?"

"I guess I thought it was you."

"Are you going to the dance?"

"I'm not sure. Are you?"

"Yes. Wanna meet me there?"

"Yeah, sure. That'd be great."

When I got off the phone, I looked in the mirror. I could

have sworn that I looked older and more masculine. I brushed my hair away from my face as if it was windblown. I practiced smiling. I rubbed my cheeks and chin to see if I needed to start shaving.

BEN

The one exception to being grounded was History Fair. It was like double punishment. The only person I was allowed to see was the one person I really wanted to avoid. Kaitlyn. She was tricky, too. If Mom or Pop answered the phone, she'd okay the plan with them first so I couldn't make up an excuse. I think she actually tried to call when she knew they'd be home. We must have gone to the library ten times. (Most kids did almost all of their research online, but once Kaitlyn discovered that Mom worked at the public library, she wouldn't hear of it.) I couldn't even ditch Kaitlyn and go riffle through the stacks because Mom was there keeping her eye on me.

It got to the point that I was being teased about Kaitlyn at home. N was the worst. We'd be eating dinner, and he'd say, "I saw you sitting with Kaitlyn at lunch today," and then Pop would start giving me that lecture about how I should treat my girlfriend, and Mom would say how cute she was.

When I denied it, things only got worse. One night I got furious.

"Saw you with your sweetie today," N said in a syrupy voice.

"She's *not* my sweetie."

"It's natural to like girls, Ben. You're getting to that age, you know," Mom said.

"I do like girls, just not *that* one."

"No, he *loves* her," said N.

"No I don't."

"They're always together at school," N threw in.

"She follows me around. I don't know how to get rid of her."

"That's not nice, Ben. Kaitlyn's a lovely girl."

"Kaitlyn's a pain."

"Then why were you kissing her on the PE field?"

I punched N right at the dinner table and got sent to my room. I climbed out onto the roof and raged.

BEN

Mom and Pop insisted I go to the dance since N was going. "You'll want to be involved in your school's social scene. It'll help you get to know everyone. And the dance will be your first postgrounding activity," said Mom, like I was supposed to be happy about it. I knew Kaitlyn would be there because she was the sort of girl who never missed anything.

"Can I call Mason and see if he's goin'?" I asked with resignation.

"Go ahead."

I ended up riding to the dance with Mason, David, and Rico. It was as bad as I expected. The lunchroom was decorated with cardboard stars and twinkling Christmas lights. An old guy who thought he was the disco king was playing horrible music and telling stupid jokes between songs.

Everyone asked, "Where's Kaitlyn?" when I walked in without her. Then she saw me and hung around me all night. Every time I escaped, she'd somehow find me.

She wanted me to dance with her, which I wasn't about to do. First of all, even though they call it a dance, not so many kids actually dance. Most just hang around and talk. Second, I didn't want to give Kaitlyn any ideas. "I don't dance," I said, and Mason, David, and Rico laughed. So she and her friends went off and danced with some seventh graders.

"You jealous?" asked Rico. He was only kidding but I didn't think it was funny.

"You're the jealous one, Rico." They all laughed. I could see N across the room with Allie, holding her hand and stuff. All I wanted to do was go home and stargaze on the roof.

Kaitlyn reappeared. She took my hand. I didn't know what to do. If I'd felt differently about her, I would have liked it. The look on Mason's face challenged me somehow. I pulled my hand away. "I don't like you that way," I said to her, and her eyes welled with tears. I felt bad to have hurt her feelings. But I still didn't want her holding my hand, and I was sick and tired of everyone thinking she was my girlfriend.

I guess the dance was my first date. I spent the whole night with Allie. She was so pretty—her eyes like stars. All my friends kept saying stuff like "You go, Ian!" or "You the man!" When her ride came, Allie kissed me real quick before getting in the car with those other girls.

But then, at school on Monday, she acted different. I felt like she was avoiding me, when all I wanted to do was look at her all day. Tara informed me that Allie had decided she didn't like me anymore, but that Claire did now.

"Well, I don't like Claire," I said. "Besides, what is this, musical boyfriends?"

Tara laughed, but I wasn't trying to be funny.

I was slammed by Allie's sudden change of heart. I asked my father what I should do. He sighed and ran his fingers through his hair. "Well, son . . . you know all about fishing, right?"

"Fishing?"

"Stay with me here. Many fishermen practice catch

and release—letting the fish go once they've landed it because the thrill is in the chase. It can be a lot like that in relationships, especially at your age. Once you're hooked, they let you go—then bait their hooks again in search of even bigger fish!"

BEN

Since our History Fair presentation was about the impact the railroads had on the expansion of America, I dressed as Casey Jones, the famous engineer, and Kaitlyn dressed as John Henry, the legendary steel-driver. I wore overalls and a blue-and-white-striped cap, and Kaitlyn dragged along a heavy sledgehammer. It turned out to be a good news/bad news kind of thing. The good news: we won first place in our division. The bad news: that meant we had to go to district-level competition the following month. So slick little Kaitlyn, who must not have gotten the message at the dance, told Mom it was important for us to practice and polish our presentation. I was stuck with Kaitlyn two afternoons a week.

BEN

N got sent to the principal for the first time in history. Mom even admitted that when the school called her at the library, she wondered what kind of trouble I'd gotten myself into. She and Pop had to go meet with Dr. Rosario because N and his friends Richard and Jake got caught skipping class behind the band room with a pack of cigarettes.

That night at the dinner table, Mom and Pop couldn't seem to get off that subject. "Smoking cigarettes. I sure thought you had better judgment than that, Ian," said Pop. I silently agreed with him. I could think of much more exciting things to get suspended over.

"Sorry." N was looking down at his spaghetti like he thought it might get up and dance.

"And you know the dangers of smoking," Mom said. "I'm surprised at you."

"We weren't gonna smoke 'em. They weren't even lit."

"A mere technicality. Jake had a lighter in his hand when Coach Ferrell found you there."

"We were just fooling around."

"Skipping class, smoking cigarettes!"

"We weren't smoking."

"You owe Mrs. Devereaux an apology. Her class is just as important as any other."

"Yes, ma'am."

"And now you're suspended for three days!"

"Your mother and I are certainly disappointed in you, Ian." Pop used that same voice the president uses in the State of the Union address.

I sat there, quiet, surprised at what I had discovered about myself. All those years when I'd gotten in trouble, I'd wished someone else had been taking the heat, but I didn't like hearing N get slammed. I decided I'd rather be the person on the firing line than the one in the audience.

BEN

Mason thought my kingdom was the most fascinating place he'd ever seen. He especially liked my da Vinci wings. He even wanted to try them out, but when I told him about their failure, we decided to leave them hanging from the rafters.

"This attic is huge. Is it scary sleeping up here?" he asked.

"No. Not scary at all. I like it."

"All that stuff piled over there sure casts freaky shadows everywhere."

"I'm used to it."

"Why don't you organize it? Stack it all in one corner or against that back wall?"

"It used to be more orderly. Every time I redo it, people come looking for something, or drag some old piece of junk up here, and before I know it, it's trashed again."

"Well, let's clean it up. I'll help you."

"Okay, thanks." While we were working, I told Mason about the meanest thing N ever did to me. It happened during our semester break last year. He's lucky I forgave him.

* * *

To get into my kingdom, I have to go through N's room and into the closet. He was moody one day and told me to stay off his property. I was working on something and kept going back and forth from my kingdom to the barn. Every time I passed through N's space, he snarled, even threw shoes at me. Maybe I *did* make a few extra runs through there just to rile him, but it was all in good clean fun. When I came in carrying a hammer and an old coffee can full of nuts, bolts, and screws, N nailed me with his soccer ball, knocking that rusty can and that hammer out of my hands. There was hardware flying everywhere.

"Pick 'em up," I snarled.

"You pick 'em up. You dropped 'em."

"It's your fault. You've gotta help."

"You pick 'em up or I'll smash your ugly face."

"No way," I said, and I ran into the closet and up the stairway to heaven.

I expected N to follow me and bust me a couple of good ones, but he didn't. Instead, he closed my folding attic stairs and nailed them shut. By the time I realized what he was doing it was too late to stop him. For hours, I kept banging on the floor (or ceiling, depending upon your geographical location), but it didn't do any good. Mom and Pop were at work, and N wasn't about to let me out. He just kept laughing and shouting stuff about political prisoners in the Tower of London. It started thundering and lightning, and rain was slashing at the windows, so I couldn't even go on the roof.

N timed it exactly right. He yanked those nails just minutes before Mom came home from work. "You tell and you're a dead man," he said. And I didn't tell because I knew he meant business.

I wasn't stupid, though. I wasn't ever going to let him have control like that again. I went into the barn and riffled through the wood scraps in an old crate. I found some sturdy one-by-twos. I cut them into foot-long segments and drilled holes in the ends. Then I strung them on some good strong line, tying knots between them. That's how I made a rope ladder—an alternate means of departure, should I ever again need one.

IAN

I tried to act confident when I got on the bus the first day of high school, but I probably looked like the nervous freshman that I was. My stop was one of the last on the route, so when I climbed to the top of the bus steps, I was greeted by a sea of hostile faces. I tried to spot a familiar or welcoming one. None. No empty seats, either. Most were already occupied by two or three people. I walked down the aisle to where only one guy was sitting. He slung his backpack in the empty space next to him. "Reserved," he growled. Four rows away was another mostly vacant seat. The punked-out girl sitting there glared at me, but I had to sit somewhere, so I joined her anyway. "Hi," I said, adopting the friendly approach.

"School sucks," she muttered, turning her face to the window. I decided the friendly approach wasn't the thing after all. I finally spotted a few kids I knew from middle school. A couple were laughing and talking, but most looked as intimidated as I was.

"Hey, Keith," I called once I'd filed from the bus. Keith

Waits had gone to my middle school. We weren't exactly friends, but at least I knew him.

"Ian—do you know where to go? I missed orientation."

"Homeroom. But you're W and I'm D, so we won't be in the same one."

He dug his schedule out of the pocket of his obviously brand-new jeans. "Room 236. Where's that?"

"Probably near 212. That's where I'm going. Come on."

We parted ways when we finally found the 200 hallway. I opened the door of 212 and walked in. The room was already crowded. A perky little blond woman greeted me with "Good morning. What's your name?" When I told her, she looked at her seating chart and pointed to a spot. The "school sucks" girl from the bus was in the seat next to mine. "Hi again," I said, sitting down.

"This place sucks."

Two classes later, she reappeared in my Spanish class. "We meet again," I said dryly. She rolled her eyes.

Then, in geometry, in the seat behind me, there was Ms. School Sucks. "Are you stalking me, or what?" I asked sarcastically.

To my surprise, she laughed. "You're the one stalking me. I was here first. But if you're going to be my stalker, I may as well introduce myself . . . I'm Mary Catherine."

"I'm Ian."

"I'll just call you Stalker, seeing as you have that tendency."

I never would have predicted that my first high school friend would be a girl with angry eyes, purple hair, pierced eyebrows, and a traditional name like Mary Catherine.

BEN

Other than Mason, all my friends thought I was kidding about my wings. They thought I was theatrical. They'd say stuff like, "Oh, Icarus, he's great. He's got the wildest imagination of anyone I know." Then, when I insisted that I really, really had wings, they'd laugh all the louder and say they wished they had my imagination. I guess that's about when I knew I shouldn't tell people about my wings. They'd either respond like those guys at school or they'd be ready to have me committed. Some things I learned to just keep to myself, or share only with Mason or N. It's a lonely world when you have to shield your soul and destiny—when you have to hide your true self away like some secret but dangerous treasure.

IAN

Ben's the best friend I ever had. He brought magic into my life. He made me see things I'd never have seen if not for him.

One day, I went up to his lair. There he was, bent over his work at a table by the window. Not his shrine table—a different one—the one I got for him from the Sinclairs' trash heap. He called it his work table. Ben had tweezers and a magnifying glass and fingernail scissors scattered on the tabletop. He was carefully dissecting an old wasps' nest, taking it apart layer by layer, and drawing and writing in a composition book every now and then. I watched him from the hatchway for a while. Finally, I said, "Icarus, what are you doing?"

"Come 'ere, N," he said, not looking up.

I sat beside him, watching him work. He was absolutely fascinated with the magic (his word) of creation those tiny wasps had harnessed by making their home.

"Feel it," he said, handing me a flake of wasps' nest that he had been rubbing between his thumb and forefinger. It felt fragile, almost like the rice paper we had used the year before in school to do printmaking.

"Smell it," directed Ben, handing me a large section of nest. It smelled dusky and dangerous.

I picked up Ben's composition book. He had glued a sheet of white drawing paper over the marbleized cardboard cover. On it he had written, "My Observations, by Icarus Delaney."

I opened the book and leafed through it. Everything was written or drawn in pencil or colored pencil. On the first page was a life-sized drawing of a dragonfly, delicately enhanced with splashes of color.

Beneath the drawing, Ben had carefully printed technical data about the dragonfly. He had measured the wingspan, the length of the body, and the length of each body segment—the head, the thorax, the abdomen. He had recorded where and when he found the dragonfly.

Below that technical section, Ben's personal observations were recorded. These started out in the same careful printing used above but quickly deteriorated to spontaneous and hurried cursive. Here Ben described the textures and colors and smells of the insect. His words gave the insect all of the mystery and magic of a being with a soul.

I turned the page. A broken shard of seashell was drawn there in soft yellows, pinks, oranges, and browns. Ben had used the same format as on the previous page—technical data, followed by poetic impressions.

Page after page demanded that I *really look* at things I'd only glanced at before. I finally understood why Ben called these simple things treasures. There was a purity to them, an innocence, an infinite beauty. There was also an order to these things, a complexity.

I picked up the shell of a cicada. It was a translucent brown color, its legs and body stiff and rigid. Ben pointed out the slit in its back where the metamorphosed insect had emerged, leaving behind its earthbound skin. "So you see," said Ben. "It does happen. It can happen."

I knew he was talking about himself and his own not-yet-emergent wings. I felt a bitter sadness for my brother, who had waited all his life for what would never happen; for what could never happen; who believed so firmly that he would sprout wings and ascend into the sky.

I fingered some of his other treasures: a snakeskin, tissue thin and delicate; a pelican wing bone, deceptively light for its size; a hawk feather with its variegated markings.

Ben picked up the hawk feather and twirled it between his thumb and forefinger. "This was a gift from my enemy, Gravity," he said. "I was watching a hawk stalk a mocking-bird, when it lost a feather, and Gravity brought it right to me. Do you think Gravity hates those creatures that can defy him?"

"Icarus, I don't think Gravity has a will, or power, or emotions, or any of that stuff. Gravity is not God, and not the devil. Gravity is just a natural force."

"But that's just your opinion, right? And you can't prove your opinion any more than I can prove mine, so what makes yours right and mine wrong?"

"Mine is based on centuries of science and physics and experimentation. Yours is based on emotion."

"Like believing in God, then?" he asked, or stated. I'm not sure which it was.

"It's different, Icarus."

"How?"

"Belief in God is based on faith."

"You mean believing in what you cannot prove?"

"Yes, because you can feel it somehow."

"Well, I have faith in my beliefs. Are yours more valid than mine because they're more widespread?"

"Maybe my beliefs are more sensible," I said, and even as I said it, I felt like a hypocrite, because really, what is sensible about faith?

"Maybe," said Ben. He put down the hawk feather and reached for the tweezers, which he used to peel another layer from the wasps' nest.

BEN

Midway through seventh grade, I decided Mason must have lost his mind. "Kaitlyn still likes you, you know," he said one day when we were sitting on the roof outside my kingdom.

"Barf," I responded.

"She's not so bad."

"She's not so great."

"Why don't you ask her to go skating Friday night? A lot of us are going."

"Are you crazy? I don't wanna go skatin', 'specially not with her." I threw a stick from the roof and watched Gravity greedily snatch it to the ground.

"She's cute, ya know?"

"Then you take her skating."

He sighed in exasperation. "It's *you* she's crazy about. But lots of guys would love to go out with her."

"Well, not me. So let's change the subject. Now."

BEN

During middle school, my back was itching all the time, morning, noon, and night. That itching even woke me up when I was sleeping because it was so relentless. I kept a hairbrush on the bookcase next to my bed just so I could scratch myself. I'd tell N to scratch and dig in with his fingernails. I'd even back up to the trunk of our live oak tree and wiggle around so the bark could ease my itching

That itching was fiercely uncomfortable, but I put up with it because I knew it was a sign. It meant something was happening with my wings; those wings trapped in the cocoon of my skin, just waiting for the right moment to emerge. The rest of me was sure changing then—my voice, my face, my body.

I was excited, expectant. I rummaged around in the linen closet at the end of the hall and found a jar of cocoa butter. Every night, N would rub it on my itchy back. I thought it might help things along. Get this—N made me pay him. Yep . . . fifty cents a night. That's three dollars and fifty cents a week. It added up. Pretty soon my money jar was drained dry, and I had to do extra chores around the house or in the yard just to pay N.

One night, I woke up with moonlight streaming through my window and my back itching worse than ever. I grabbed that hairbrush off the bookcase and started scratching away as if I was a mangy dog.

Suddenly it hit me like a freight train. What if I had damaged my wings by all that scratching? I felt sick—thought I was going to throw up. I visualized my reptilian wings unfolding like proud flowers, beautiful and magic except for all those punctures and rips caused by the bristles of that brush. Wouldn't that have been an awful sight?

Throwing the hairbrush across the room like it was a venomous serpent, I hoped and prayed I hadn't damaged my wings. I worried about it all the time. N would bait me, telling me my wings were poking out and they were all torn up. So I'd run to the mirror all panicked and realize he was just lying. I had dreams. Horrible dreams, of me standing on a precipice with my tattered wings, unable to take flight. I'd awaken from those dreams with my stomach tied in monkeys' fists. I knew, really knew, that one day I would fly, and I truly had only one goal, one dream—flight.

Turns out, my wings weren't ready to emerge then. Probably it was just some kind of inner-wing metamorphosis causing my back to itch so.

Ben made a sign that he hung on the closet wall. It was one of those red circles with a diagonal line cutting across it, like a NO SMOKING sign. Except Ben's sign said NO GRAVITY and had a picture of a knife falling blade-first inside the circle. For Ben, Gravity always began with a capital G. Ben hated Gravity the way lots of kids hate homework or bedtime. Or worse. The way flagrant Republicans hate liberals. The way politicians hate scandals. The way street racers hate radar guns.

Ben sometimes raved about the injustice of Gravity. All of my arguments about natural law and physics just made Ben even madder. For Ben, Gravity wasn't a natural phenomenon. Gravity was a breathing, vicious rival. Hungry and greedy and strong.

BEN

The first week of eighth grade, I got into a fight with a boy from school. The only person I'd ever fought with before was N, and fighting with your brother is different. It doesn't really mean anything. This kid, Creighton Rice, had been ragging me since sixth grade because people called me Icarus. I didn't care if he disliked my name, but no one was going to hassle me incessantly and get away with it. Especially not a loser like Creighton Rice.

Mason, David, and I were cutting across the parking lot of the deserted office building across the street from school. As we waited for the light to change, I heard a weaselly voice squeaking "Oh, look, it's Icky-pus Delaney. Icky, Icky, Icky-pus!"

"Hang on," I said to Mason and David. I walked over to Creighton. Stood right in front of him and looked him square in the eyes. "You're gonna shut up and leave me alone from now on."

He took a step back. "Says who?"

I stepped toward him. "Says me."

People were gathering around us. "Kick his butt, Delaney," I heard someone yell.

"You gonna shut your big ugly mouth, Rice?"

"You gonna make me, Icky-pus?"

All in one motion, I slid my backpack to the ground, kicked it out of my way, grabbed the front of Creighton's shirt, got right up in his face, and snarled, "Yeah, I'm gonna make you." Then I shoved him hard, and he stumbled backward about three steps before sprawling on his rear. In spite of my inexperience, I somehow knew the unwritten fighting rules, so I took a step toward him and stood there awaiting his next move. I was hoping he'd back off, but he didn't. He got up and lunged at me. We both crashed to the ground, grasping and thrashing and punching. I don't know how long that went on—it seemed a long time but Mason later said it was pretty quick—before someone yanked me off him and drew me away. Once my eyes cleared, I realized it was Mr. Spanier, who taught seventh-grade English. He was saying something, but my ears were buzzing, so I didn't hear him. I saw Coach Ferrell pulling Creighton up, and suddenly I was aware of the ring of kids surrounding us. Mr. Spanier and Coach Ferrell dragged us across the street to school. Some of the kids followed, but most of them clustered in small groups, and I knew they were discussing the fight.

They took us to the principal's office, but she wasn't there. I heard the secretary paging her: "Dr. Rosario, we need you in your office."

"You—over there," Coach Ferrell said to me, and he motioned to the chair near the window. "And you—there." Looking at Creighton, he gestured to the seat beside the door.

I was surprised to see Creighton's lip bleeding and his left eye already starting to swell. I felt bruised and battered myself, but I wasn't about to show any sign of weakness, so I resisted the urge to probe the throbbing places on my face and body.

Creighton started rapidly babbling his version of the events, but Coach Ferrell told him to be quiet and wait for Dr. Rosario. Mr. Spanier handed me the phone. "Call your parents." He turned to Creighton. "And when he's done, you call yours." As I dialed, I glared at Creighton. He glared back at me.

So my parents came, as did his, and after a lot of lecturing and threats, Dr. Rosario made a point of saying, "Zero tolerance means zero tolerance, and the only thing preventing you two boys from expulsion is a loophole. You're lucky the fight didn't occur on school property. But understand, boys. This *is* your last chance. Now go."

No one said anything on the ride home. Mom's shoulders were rigid, and Pop kept running his fingers through his hair. When we got to the house, I caught it with both barrels. The usual drill about fights not solving anything, and sticks and stones, and how I'd let them down. And I got grounded. No TV, no computer, no telephone, no nothing.

I know in books and movies, people often become friends after they get into a fight, but it wasn't that way with Creighton and me. We avoided each other for the most part. I'm not sure who technically won the fight, but he never called me Icky-pus again. He didn't end up going to my high school. Neither did Kaitlyn. I considered myself lucky on both counts at the time.

We had a family reunion at the beach the summer before Ben started high school. My mother's entire family was there. Everyone stayed in little pink cottages in the same motel complex.

Things got off to a bad start. All of the relatives were gathered at Uncle Eddie's cottage when my brother told everyone that his name wasn't Ben anymore, it was Icarus. My mother turned twelve shades of red and said firmly, "His name is Ben."

"But call me Icarus," insisted Ben.

"No, call him Ben," she returned. Everyone was quiet. Even the babies recognized the declaration of war in my mother's voice. "Frank," she said to my father, "why don't you take *Ben* for a walk?" That meant my father was supposed to reason with Ben, which was like reasoning with a paperweight. I never could figure out why she hated for Ben to be called Icarus so much.

Ben shrugged, and he and my father left the cottage.

*　*　*

Here's the thing about Ben—he wouldn't argue with my father or mother, but he wouldn't change his mind, either. He'd just let them say their piece, then he'd follow his own stars. So usually it was a stalemate.

All of the cousins called Ben Icarus, and all of the aunts and uncles called Icarus Ben, and my mother and Ben hardly spoke to each other. Ben avoided her by waking up early and slipping out of the cottage until dinnertime. If she heard someone say "Icarus," she'd say "Ben" in a strong voice.

One day, Uncle Joey rented a catamaran and took Ben and me sailing. The boat cut through the water and caught the wind, rising from the ocean balanced on one pontoon. The sail snatched the wind and swallowed its power. We used our bodies to keep the boat from capsizing, leaning way out over the side, laughing and thrilled. (We had a little help from Gravity, but Ben would never admit that.) We sailed for hours and hours, and Uncle Joey taught us the principles that allow man to harness the wind. It was great, in spite of getting sunburned. "Almost like flying," Ben said, smiling really big. "Almost like flying." His eyes looked far away, and his voice was soft and dreamy.

Aunt Anna had brought old home videos to the reunion with her. Many of them had been made before I was born. We were watching them one night, and I was surprised when I saw my parents on the screen. My father seemed about the same in looks and personality, just a little younger. But my mother wasn't just young and beautiful—she had charisma! Her blue eyes flashed with promise and her smile made me want to hear the sound of her voice. In fact, her energy level reminded me of Ben's. For the first time, I saw a strong connection between them. Her gestures and subtleties were mirrors of Ben's.

I wondered if Ben saw those elusive similarities? Or my father? For that matter, did my mother see them? Is that what scared her so much about Ben? Had she herself harbored secret fantasies? Delusions? Mysteries? Had she buried them away deep inside so that she would appear sedate and composed?

I looked across the room and watched as she viewed the videos. She sat next to my father, her head resting on his shoulder. She didn't really *look* different—it was more her aura that had changed, and her eyes. I wondered if she felt exposed, having an electronic image reveal that she had another story, another side, another existence.

I turned my gaze to Ben, who was sitting on the floor with our cousins, Sasha and Andrew. He wasn't even watching the tape. He was looking at his hand and I saw that he held a beetle. He was observing it as it crawled on his palm. It was blackly iridescent in the electric blue light of the TV screen.

BEN

I was sidelined during a soccer game in one of my ninth-grade PE classes so I clowned around with a couple of other guys doing cartwheels and flips and tricks. The diving coach saw me. Next thing I knew, he and my PE coach were signaling me over. I wondered how I'd gotten myself in trouble this time.

"I'm Coach LaGrange. You're not bad ... flipping around over there. I run the diving team. Have you ever done any diving?"

"Not really. I mean, I cut up and stuff, but I don't know how to do it right."

"Think you can learn?"

"I guess."

"Come to my office. I'll get you the releases and health forms. First practice is Monday at three-thirty. Be there. I think you've got potential."

I looked at my PE coach questioningly. "Well, go on," he said.

The first day of diving practice I felt like a fool. I wore my blue and green board shorts, while all these other guys were in little tiny Speedos. "Do I have to wear one of those?" I asked the coach.

"Only at meets. What you're wearing now is fine for practice."

I suddenly wished I hadn't come. Those guys couldn't have looked more naked if they'd *been* naked.

"So who are you?" asked one of the older guys. He was tall and very thin.

"Icarus Delaney."

"Can you dive?"

"I dunno."

"Rookie alert . . . rookie alert . . . ," he started chanting. The other guys all laughed. There were girls there, too. The guys might have been mostly naked in those Speedos, but the girls all wore one-piece swimmer bathing suits with high necks. They still looked pretty good to me, though.

A girl with a long braid down her back walked over to me. "Are you related to Ian Delaney?"

"He's my brother."

"Ian's always been in lots of my classes. He's all right."

"Yeah. He's okay most of the time."

She laughed. "I'm Sarah Quentin. I'll help you out today. And just ignore those guys. They think they're all that."

That first day, I practiced jumping. Yeah, jumping. Something I'd been doing since I was a baby. And Coach LaGrange actually said I did it right a couple of times.

IAN

When I found out that Sarah Quentin was on the diving team, I was more than happy to become Ben's chauffeur. I always went early to pick him up. I wasn't about to miss the opportunity to see Sarah in a bathing suit. She often stayed late to teach Ben new moves. His skills improved quickly, and I gave Sarah a ride home, so it worked out great for everyone.

Before long, I was dropping Ben off first, then taking Sarah home. It reached the point that we didn't even use Ben as an excuse anymore. I really liked being with Sarah. She was fun and smart and nice. She liked me, too. A lot.

Ben got arrested when he was fifteen. The phone rang late in the night, and I heard my parents' voices in their room. I could tell by the quiet tremor in my mother's tone that something was up.

I rolled out of bed, yanked on my jeans, and stumbled down the hall to their room. "What's going on?" I asked, leaning on the doorjamb.

"Go back to bed, Ian," said my mother softly.

"No. Get dressed and come with me. Your brother is at the police station," said my father.

"Icarus?" I asked, puzzled, because I thought he was asleep in his kingdom.

"Ben!" barked my mother. "His name is Ben. Not Icarus!"

"Why's he at the police station?" I asked, addressing my father and wondering what Ben could possibly have done.

"Something about trespassing. Go get dressed." My father was buttoning his shirt as he spoke.

I went to my room, grabbed a T-shirt and my flip-flops, then went back down the hall. "Ready?"

My father snatched his keys off the dresser. "Yeah, let's go." He kissed my mother on the forehead. "Everything will be fine, Olivia. Try to get some sleep."

"G'night, Mom," I said.

I followed my father down the stairs and out to his truck. It was a beautiful night, spangled with stars and with just a kiss of a breeze. I got into the truck and changed the radio station to the one that Ben and I liked. My father turned the volume all the way down. "I can't handle that right now, Ian," he said, running the fingers of his left hand through his hair.

"What'd Icarus do?" I asked as he turned onto the highway and shifted gears.

"Look Ian, I don't care if your brother wants to be called Santa Claus, or Blackbeard, or Elvis Presley . . . you know, a rose by any other name . . . but call him Ben around your mother. She's got enough to worry about without the two of you shoving that Icarus thing down her throat."

"I don't see why it's such a big deal. Why does she get so worked up about it?"

"You know, Ian, Ben's fun and creative and imaginative, but he hasn't been an easy kid to raise. You might not remember all of the visits to the emergency room—all of the parent-teacher conferences—all of the near disasters, but we do. You don't know how much we've worried. How many times . . . Look, just give your mother a break and don't call him Icarus in front of her anymore."

"Sure, no problem," I muttered.

We stopped for a red light. I looked at the blue-green numbers glowing on the dashboard clock. 2:44. I asked again, "What exactly did Ic—Ben—do, anyway?"

"Trespassing on the train trestle. The railroad police caught him and turned him over to the city police. He's downtown."

"In jail?"

"At the police station. I don't know if he's actually locked up."

"Who was he with?" I sifted through Ben's friends in my head, trying to guess who else might be out this late.

"I didn't think to ask. It's not every night I get a phone call telling me that my fifteen-year-old son has been arrested."

We drove along in silence. I tried to imagine Ben in jail. Had he told the guard he was going to fly away? Had he asked the other inmates to check his back for some sign of his wings?

"Since we're out late and all, can I ditch school tomorrow?" I asked my father.

"Give it a rest, Ian," he said, rubbing his chin. I could hear his whiskers protesting as he pushed them in the opposite direction from which they grew. I realized that he was more bothered by this whole situation than he wanted anyone to know. Maybe even bothered by the whole history of Ben's tragedies and delusions. I think both my parents were always worried and scared that one day Ben would fall off one edge or another (physical or mental) and never return.

At the police station, I stood next to my father while he told the man behind the counter why we were there. The man sent us down the hall to another desk, where a uniformed officer led us to a room. Ben was in the room, sitting at a table. The officer stood in the doorway. "I'll get the detective handling the case," he said, leaving.

I'd never been to the police station before. It was strange—both noisy and silent at the same time. The silence lurked beneath the noise, lonely and broken. The noise was like a thick blanket of fog, making the atmosphere somehow unpredictable, threatening, and distorted.

"Sorry, Pop," said Ben, looking into my father's eyes.

"Are you all right?" asked my father.

"Yessir."

"What happened?"

I sat down in one of the empty chairs. "Pop, sit down, why don't ya?" I said. "You can't tell someone what happened if they're hovering over your shoulder." My father pulled a chair up to the table and sat. He looked expectantly at Ben.

Ben inhaled and spoke very quietly. "I walked out on the train trestle—"

"With who?" interrupted my father.

"By myself." Ben was rolling the hem of his T-shirt between the thumb and forefinger of his left hand.

"Why?" asked my father.

"I didn't want to be with anyone else."

"I mean why did you walk out on the trestle?"

"Oh. I wanted to . . . don't get mad, Pop . . ." He looked down at his hands. "I figured it this way . . . that trestle is way high so boats and ships can go under it. So it'd be a good takeoff point, ya know, to see if my wings were ready. That's why I went there. I wasn't going to vandalize or anything stupid like that."

My father's face was ghostly. "Ben, are you listening to yourself? You're in high school. You're fifteen . . . Ben, look at me . . . you're fifteen years old, and you still think you have some kind of wings! I thought you'd gotten over all that . . . son, this isn't sane. You are a human being, and human beings do not have wings. You say you weren't going to do anything stupid? Good God, Ben, you don't call jumping off the trestle in the middle of the night stupid? Because you think you can fly? Ben . . . son . . . you scare the hell out of me." My father's voice was shaky, his eyes glassy.

"Pop, why can't you just believe?" Ben asked, and I could

see the sorrow in his eyes. It had always been agonizing for him that no one took his flying thing seriously. If he only understood how much we wished we could believe him.

My father sighed. "Ben, you can't fly. You can't," he said flatly. "And jumping off the trestle in the dead of night is no way to prove otherwise." He was speaking in a calm, reasonable voice, but I could hear panic tapping at the door. I was so glad my mother wasn't there. I think she would have broken down completely if she'd heard what Ben had been planning to do.

A police detective came into the room, and he and my father shook hands and introduced themselves. The detective sat down in the last empty chair. Ben sat up straight, but he looked at his hands resting on the tabletop.

"I guess your son told you he was trespassing on the trestle."

"Yes, he did," said my father.

"And it's way past curfew for someone his age. Are you aware of that, Mr. Delaney?"

"We had no idea he wasn't at home. He was there when I went to bed," said my father. He looked weary.

The detective cleared his throat and checked his beeper, which had just beeped. "The railroad police picked up your son. He was almost out in the middle of the trestle. Way over the water's surface. If he'd fallen, the impact would have been like landing on concrete. He probably would have died."

Ben hung his head. No one spoke. My father placed his hand on Ben's forearm.

"Naturally, the railroad police searched him. He didn't have spray paint or tools or weapons, so they really don't think he meant any harm . . . sabotage or vandalism or anything of that nature . . . but they are cracking down on trespassers since that kid got hit last year. That trestle is a dangerous place to be anytime, but especially in the middle of the night."

Of course, we couldn't tell the detective that Ben was planning to fly away. He would've had us all locked up. Finally my father spoke. "I'm sure Ben just exercised poor judgment. He should have been home. Right, Ben?"

"Yessir," said Ben.

"I checked Ben's name on the computer. He's never been in trouble before," said the detective. "Since this is the first time he's been picked up, I thought maybe he deserved a break. I spoke to the head of security at the railroad, and he said they are willing to drop the charges if you promise you won't repeat the offense." The detective looked at Ben.

"Well, Ben?" said my father.

"I won't ever do it again. I promise," Ben said softly. His voice sounded tight.

After Ben and my father signed some paperwork, we left the police station. No one said anything in the truck. The dashboard clock glowed 4:26. The roads were deserted. I'd never seen downtown so quiet.

My father pulled into an all-night diner. "Let's get some coffee and talk," he said.

We went inside. The place was empty except for two men drinking coffee at the counter. We went to sit in a booth by the window. The waitress appeared right away. "Just coffee for me. Boys, get breakfast if you want," said my father. Ben and I ordered pancakes and bacon and eggs. We sat in silence until the waitress brought us our drinks. When she walked away, my father looked across the booth at Ben. "We can't tell your mother you were trying to fly off the trestle in the middle of the night. She'd fall apart. Are you with me so far?"

"Yessir."

"I don't like to lie to her, but I just can't tell her that. I just can't." I could tell my father was close to the edge himself.

"Pop, we won't tell her. We'll just say he was out walking," I said.

"Ben, I don't want you to kill yourself. You're my son. You boys are the world to me. Don't you know that?"

"Yes," said Ben. He was looking at his hands.

"You do understand that if you'd jumped, you'd probably be dead?" My father sounded like he was speaking to a very young child. I wondered if Ben noticed; if he was offended.

"Maybe," said Ben.

"Maybe? Ben, you can't fly. You can't. You've tried before. You would have fallen into the water, probably to your death."

"Pop, if the time was right—"

"What if the time wasn't right, Ben? What then?"

"But to know, I'd have to try. Otherwise, I might never achieve my destiny."

My father sighed; sounded exasperated. Ben looked up. There were tears trapped in his eyelashes. "Ian, talk to him," my father pleaded, desperate.

"Icarus, Pop's right. You're gonna get hurt if you keep this up. None of us want to see that happen."

Ben stared at me like I was the ultimate Judas, the quintessential Benedict Arnold, the Olympic gold medalist of traitors. I felt horrible.

"Ben," said my father, "are you listening to us?"

"Yes, I'm listening." He brushed away the tears that had sneaked out of his eyes.

"And?" prodded my father.

"And you don't understand." Ben spoke so softly I could barely hear him.

My father rubbed his temples. "Well, then, son—help me

understand, because this whole thing is starting to gray my hair."

Ben gazed blankly out the window, not speaking. Finally he turned to look at us, his blue eyes lost and isolated. "I've always known . . . always"—he was now looking deeply into my father's eyes—"that I could fly. I know no one believes me. I know all of you think I'm crazy. But I've always known. Always." He was quiet, a few tears dancing down his cheeks. "I don't know when, and I don't know where or how, but it's gonna happen. I will fly. I know it."

My father and Ben locked eyes for a long time. I wanted to hug Ben, to hug my father. I wanted desperately to be able to make everything all right. My father propped his elbows on the table and dropped his face to his hands. When he looked back up, his eyes were soft and sad. "Ben, I don't understand. I'm trying, but I don't understand."

The waitress picked that moment to show up with our food. She was chattering inanely about the politics of waffles versus pancakes. It was practically surreal to hear her blathering on when we were in the midst of something frightening and weighty.

My father sipped his coffee. "I'd better go call your mother. She's probably panicking by now." He walked away, digging in his pocket for change for the pay phone.

I looked at my brother. "Icarus, you're killing them with all this flying stuff. You know that, don't you?"

"N, it's who I am. Why doesn't anyone see that?" He dropped his fork and pushed his plate away. "Nobody gets it. Not one person in the whole world gets it." He turned his face to the window. I could see tears streaming down his cheeks, reflected in the glass. "Sometimes I feel like I'm totally alone on this planet."

I could taste his isolation. Still, I persisted. "Well, Icarus, what if I thought I could swim like a fish? So people kept

121

having to yank me out of the water and pump the ocean from my lungs. But I kept insisting I was aquatic. Would that make sense to you?"

"Yeah, it would. It would if you said that you knew in your blood and your bones and your soul that you were supposed to be a fish. I'd want you to *be* who you were. I'd want to see your fins shimmering in the sunlight when you glided to the water's surface."

"And if I drowned in this pursuit?"

"But you wouldn't, N, would you, if that's who you *really* were?"

"But you've jumped before, Icarus, many times, and never sprouted wings."

"They weren't ready yet."

"They may never be ready. And lots of those times it was only luck that kept you alive. Even tonight, you could have died."

"Or I could have flown."

"Ben, things are starting to come undone at home, and if you keep—"

My father slipped back into the booth, talking as he sat. "Your mother and I decided that neither of you should go to school today. It's been a long night." He looked at Ben's untouched food in the center of the table. "Not eating?"

"Sorry, Pop. Lost my appetite. Guess I'm too tired."

BEN

I was sure I'd get grounded and have to quit the diving team after my incident with the police. Instead, Mom bought me the official team uniform, a blue and gold Speedo. At the first meet I felt so obvious. The top halves of my legs were stark white since my tan stopped where my board shorts started—around my knees. It didn't help that Mason and N were in the stands whistling and catcalling me. There I stood on the diving board, practically naked in that microscopic Speedo, doing my amateur dives, while those other guys were performing these fabulous tricks.

Sarah must've guessed how I felt, because she drew me aside and said, "Icarus, be patient. You have potential. This is all new to you. And all the girls think you look hot in your Speedo!" I must've blushed fifteen shades of red when she said that. I knew she wasn't coming on to me, because she and N were tight, but still . . .

The judges scored me decently on the three dives I actually did: a front dive, a back dive, and an inward. But it seemed to me that everyone else had an entire repertoire of dives.

Sarah sat with me at our postperformance meeting. "So what if Jason Brinkman did get those great scores? He's still a jerk. And he looks skank in a Speedo."

IAN

My father was reading on the front porch. It was late. My mother was asleep and I don't know what Ben was doing. "You busy?" I asked.

"What . . . no. Just reading. What's up?"

"Nothing really . . . thought we could talk."

"Sure." He yanked a dead leaf from a potted plant and used it to mark his page. Then he laid the book on the porch rail.

I sat on the swing. "Pretty night." That wasn't what I wanted to say, but I had to start somewhere.

"Yes, it is. Beautiful moon."

"Yeah . . . Pop, I've been wondering, what was Mom like when you met her?"

He smiled. "Magic. She was like no one I'd ever known. I couldn't believe it when she agreed to go out with me."

"But was she different?"

"Different?"

"Than she is now."

"I'm not sure what you mean."

"At the family reunion, remember Aunt Anna brought those old videos? Mom seemed so different. So energized and sparkly."

"You don't see that in her now?" he asked after a pause.

"Not like that . . . Pop, she reminded me of Ben. You know, all jazzed and lively. She's not really like that now."

"Maybe she is, Ian. Maybe you just don't see it."

"Do you?"

"I do. But I can see how you wouldn't. When I was your age, I thought anyone over twenty-five was simply going through the motions. I didn't get it that adults can love or suffer or delight just as deeply, painfully, and intensely as teenagers. I thought when you reached a certain age, your life was set in stone, and stagnant. But Ian, that's not true. I know that now, from this side of the line. The very young and the very old and everyone in between have dreams and secrets and heartbreaks."

"So what are her dreams, her secrets, her heartbreaks?"

"Perhaps you should ask her, son. She's a beautiful woman, inside and out. To you, she's old and motherly, but not to me. To me, she's still magic."

BEN

"I'm really surprised you didn't get in more trouble over the trestle thing," Mason said.

"Me too. N got it worse when he got suspended back in eighth grade."

"You weren't *really* gonna jump, were you?"

"Fly, Mason, fly."

"But Icarus—"

"Mason, you know all about my wings."

"Yeah. But if I were you, I'd wait for 'em to finish morphing before I did something that dangerous."

"Maybe. Or maybe some cataclysmic event is what's needed. . . ."

"Be patient, Icarus. Recklessness rarely helps any situation. No point in killing yourself."

"You sound like my father."

"Sorry."

BEN

N and I talked Mom into buying us surfboards. Even though Pop never gave her specifics about my night on the trestle, I thought she sensed I was getting itchy. Maybe she was hoping I'd find riding the waves just as satisfying as riding the wind.

I couldn't stop thinking about the trestle, though . . . wondering if my destiny had been thwarted. Only now, I couldn't do it . . . jump, that is—I had promised Pop—but that trestle was like a magnet. Drawing me. It was the perfect place . . . the best one I'd ever seen.

I found myself going there—not out on the trestle where I might get arrested again, but just to the base of it, where I sat and wondered. It was high, gracefully arcing skyward as it neared the ship channel. There was so much sky there, so much air, so much space. . . .

Anyway, Mom got us these surfboards, and we started surfing a lot. We weren't fabulous like the guys in surf flicks, but we did all right. I liked being on my own out in the water, unless you counted Gravity. He was always there, everywhere I went, everything I did, clawing at my heels like a hungry shadow, so he didn't count any more than my breath did.

It would take more than a surfboard, though, to turn me away from my destiny.

Aunt Anna came to stay with Ben and me when our parents went to Maine for a forestry convention. Ben and I, at fifteen and seventeen, thought we were old enough to stay by ourselves, but my mother said leaving two teenage boys unsupervised for a week was a recipe for certain disaster. My father agreed with her. If we had to have a babysitter, at least it was Aunt Anna. She's my favorite aunt. Even when I was really little, she always talked to me like we were equals.

One night, Ben and I sat with her in the living room. "It's too bad your mother quit painting. I always loved her work." She was looking at the painting hanging over the piano. "Such great lines . . . so expressive . . ."

I glanced at Ben, who was gazing at the painting hanging over the mantelpiece. "I like 'em, too," he said. "It's the colors— the way they work against each other. The way they jump before my eyes."

"She really could manipulate color. Even the critics said that."

"Critics? Was she famous?" I asked.

"Well, locally renowned, I'd say. She did lots of shows in the area, and the galleries loved to get their hands on her work."

"Why'd she quit?" I walked to the fireplace, studying the painting above it.

"I don't know . . . marriage, kids, work, life. She never thought she was good enough to make a living at it, but she was. I told her that. So she took that job at the library, saying she'd paint on the side. But as time went on, her fever burned itself out. I don't think she's painted in years, has she?"

"No. But I wish she would," said Ben.

Aunt Anna sighed. "Your father would like that, too. He told me it was exciting for him to see the images emerge when she was working. He said her paintings unlocked her secrets for him."

The next day, Ben dragged some of Mom's paintings from the attic and lined the hallways with them, creating a gallery. For the rest of the week, he'd take a painting from the wall, lean it against the sofa, sit across the room from it, and study it. Aunt Anna and I joined him sometimes. We talked in soft, respectful voices about the brushstrokes, the colors, the nuances. If it hadn't been for Aunt Anna and Ben, I might never have really looked at my mother's paintings. They had always been part of my surroundings, so I guess I took them for granted.

IAN

Sarah was Ben's mentor on the diving team, and because of her, all the girls started hanging around Ben at practice and meets, which made all the guys hang around Ben, too. Suddenly, my brother was one of the most popular kids on the team.

I always went to the meets. My parents usually went as well, but I rarely sat with them. I'd go to the section in the stands where the other kids from school gathered. Sarah was as graceful as a ballerina on the diving board. I loved watching her. Even on the rare occasions that she messed up badly enough to hit the water with a loud slap and lots of splash, she was beautiful.

Ben's skills improved quickly. By midseason, he was able to do some of the more advanced dives. He told me diving was almost what he imagined flying would be like when he got his wings. I wondered when he was going to finally outgrow that whole ridiculous flying obsession and join the rest of us on planet Earth. Even so, I was glad he made the diving team because that's what got Sarah and me together.

Mary Catherine ditched her punk look and went for a Marilyn Monroe style in our junior year. She bleached her hair a blinding platinum and always wore colorful dresses that emphasized her small waist and curvy hips. The bright red lipstick she wore completed the package. Guys who had ridiculed her Billy Idol appearance couldn't get enough of her new persona.

"It's so funny. Those guys acted like I was diseased or something, and now . . . can you believe it, Stalker? Ron Blakely asked me out! Not that I'd go, but Ron Blakely?" Ron Blakely was the ultimate preppie in our school. He drove a Volvo, and most of his clothing was emblazoned with ABERCROMBIE & FITCH.

Mary Catherine never dated any one guy. "It would be like having the same thing for dinner every night!" she said. "Variety, Stalker, variety!"

"Are you and your date still going to prom with Sarah and me?"

"Yeah. I'm going with my brother's friend, Matt. Wait'll

you see my dress. I got it at a vintage clothing store, and it's straight out of the 1950s. I'm gonna beehive my hair. Matt got a Cary Grant–looking smoking jacket to wear."

"I hope you don't mind if Sarah and I are a little more typical."

"Not at all, Stalker. I expected nothing less."

BEN

N quit seeing Sarah at the end of the school year. I didn't get it. She seemed perfect to me. He always looked happy when they were together. He tried to explain it to me. "Variety, Icarus, variety! I don't wanna be with just one person all the time. It's like eating the same thing for dinner every night."

I felt caught in the middle. Sarah was my friend, but N was my brother. Sarah pulled me aside a few times with questions that I couldn't answer because to do so would betray N, even if I did think he was making a major mistake.

N got irritated that Sarah and I remained friends. It made him uncomfortable. Maybe he thought he was our only topic of conversation, but he wasn't. Actually, he was the topic to be avoided. I even told Sarah that, and she understood.

I got a job lifeguarding at the local pool the summer before my senior year of high school. I spent a lot of time blowing my whistle and saying "No running" to little kids, and reminding people that they were supposed to shower before they got in the pool, but overall it was a pretty cushy job. Who could complain about sunshine and girls in bikinis? Besides, lifeguards got to take lots of breaks.

Sometimes Ben would come to practice his diving. Usually he did more goofy tricks than anything else. My coworkers all liked him.

This girl named Marta started coming to the pool almost every day. She was one grade beneath me at school, and she'd caught my eye before. She was really hot and must have had a whole closetful of minuscule bikinis.

When I was on break, I'd go sit with Marta. She started waiting until we closed the pool at night so I could bring her home. We didn't usually go straight home, though. We knew all kinds of places we could go and not get bothered by anyone.

BEN

One summer night, Mom dropped me off at the pool. "Ian will bring you home when he gets off." I practiced my dives and played water polo with a bunch of other guys.

I noticed Marta hanging on the legs of N's lifeguard stand when he was on duty—following him into the office when he was on break. Marta was real pretty, but there was something about her that bothered me. She was so plastic, always playing to her audience.

When the pool closed, Marta hung all over N on the way to the car. I felt embarrassed to be there. She kept touching him and kissing his ear.

"We're going to grab something to eat. Wanna come, Icarus?" N asked.

Before I could answer, Marta said, "Oh, I'm sure he's tired, Ian. We can take him home first."

"I can do that," said N, and I hated him then, because he let her treat me like I was invisible. "Home, Icarus, or do you wanna join us?"

"Home," I answered flatly.

The rest of the drive, N was overly cheerful and tried to have conversations with me, like he knew he'd been a jerk and felt bad about it. But he still let it happen.

And Marta did everything she could to shut me out and let me know I was excess baggage.

BEN

At the first diving team practice my sophomore year, I wore my Speedo. I was used to it by then. And I'd worn it to a deserted area at the beach a few times over the summer so my upper legs weren't blindingly white this time around. The new guys all stood out like sore thumbs in their bathing suits and board shorts. Sarah was there, her long hair braided for practice as usual.

"Hello, Icarus. Did you have a good summer?" She hugged me.

"Good enough. What about you?"

"Good enough . . . how's Ian?"

"Okay. He worked at the pool all summer."

"I know. I saw him there the one time I went to practice my dives . . . with Marta Markowitz hanging all over him. I went to the pool at the university after that."

"They have a nice pool."

"I hear Ian's still going out with Marta."

"Yeah."

"You like her?"

"She's all right. I like you better."

She smiled at me. "You're so sweet. But I'm over it, Icarus. Life goes on."

IAN

When I started seeing Marta exclusively, Ben asked me, "Whatever happened to variety, N? Seems to me you're having the same thing for dinner every night, followed by heartburn."

"Maybe what I'm having is dessert. And at least I'm not suffering from famine."

Still, even though I'd never let him know it, I understood what he meant. Being with Marta had its good points, but at times I still felt shackled and strangled—something I'd never felt with Sarah.

BEN

I wrote a story for my literature class. I'll share the abridged version here.

Long ago, there evolved two similar races. One is known today as the human race, called ground-dwellers in previous times, and the other was a race of winged bipeds. These two races had a parallel evolutionary path, but specialization gave wings to only one of them—the flyers. The two races lived peacefully together, sharing common goals, inbreeding, coexisting. But over time the ground-dwellers became envious and suspicious of the beauty and power of the flyers' wings. What began as petty prejudices escalated into serious bigotry, and finally resulted in the brutal massacres of the flyers. Realizing that their survival depended upon retreat, the remaining flyers migrated to a lush island in an uncharted sea, where they built a utopian society of intelligent, peaceful people.

As time passed, the ground-dwellers forgot their winged brothers, and history and legend merged to the point that the idea of winged people became ludicrous. Humans became absorbed in other pursuits—the pursuits of wealth, power, sex, and technology.

But remember, the two very similar species had inbred in earlier times. The gene for wings was recessive, often skipping many generations before asserting itself in the ground-dwellers. The flyers of ground-dweller parentage weren't born with wings. Morphing took place beneath the surface of such beings until the planets were properly aligned, at which time the wings burst forth and unfurled in flaming reptilian beauty. Humans abhorred and feared those wings, and amputations and murders took place. Only the occasional flyer escaped, making his way to the island kingdom of the flyers, drawn by invisible rhythms caressing the earth.

One such being meshed with the society of flyers easily, but he missed his ground-dweller family and friends. He urged the winged people to reunite with the ground-dwellers. The flyers worked quietly, in ways so subtle that the humans detected nothing. When human society became less violent, they attributed it to law enforcement. When their children seemed happier and healthier, they congratulated their social programs. When their gardens and farms flourished, they wrote of special soils and fertilizers. But their eyes were clearer, and their songs were sweeter, and their hearts were full of joy.

Then the flyers presented themselves to the ground-dwellers, laden with gifts and good wishes. Sadly, though, the ground-dwellers had bred into their souls deep suspicions and jealousies, and they tore the hearts from the breasts of the flyers and shredded their wings into bloody ribbons. They simply did not have the faith or courage to accept a species so similar to their own, yet so pure and good.

A few flyers survived, and are hidden away in some secret place even now. Perhaps one day, in some other time, they will once again emerge, and risk their lives to share the world of others. Perhaps not.

IAN

Late one night when there was no moon at all, Ben lay in the grass near our mother's vegetable garden. I went to sit beside him.

"What's up, Icarus?"

"Nothin'. Just lookin' at the stars."

"Oh . . . mind if I sit here?"

"No . . . go ahead. . . . Hey, N, have you ever wondered what it would feel like to be a beam of light—a visible thing with physical properties like warmth and refraction and reflection, but still unable to be captured or held?"

"No, Icarus, I've never thought about that."

"I wouldn't mind being light. Light can defy Gravity. If a beam of light is aimed into the sky, it never comes back down—it just keeps shooting off into space forever and ever."

"I guess," I said. I wasn't really following his reasoning.

"So is light finite or infinite?" he asked me.

"Geez, Ben, how would I know?"

We were both quiet; Ben gazing at the sky, me pulling up

blades of grass and splitting them into strips. Finally I spoke. It was about something that had been gnawing at me for a while. "Icarus, you don't like Marta, do you?"

"She's okay. She's pretty."

"But you don't like her," I repeated.

He didn't say anything.

"Why not, Icarus? Why don't you like her?" I insisted.

"N, I don't *know* her."

"Yes you do."

"Not really *know* her," he said. "She doesn't talk about anything real."

"You're here talking about being a beam of light, and you say she doesn't talk about anything real?" I asked incredulously.

"You know what I mean, N."

"No, I don't. Tell me."

He paused and turned to look at me. "She's good at talking about school, and clothes, and her friends, and her hair. But if you even try to have a conversation with her about something real, she has nothing to say."

"I have great conversations with her," I said, but in hindsight, that wasn't necessarily true. I couldn't remember ever having had a conversation with Marta that challenged my beliefs or awakened new ideas in me.

"About what?" asked Ben.

"We talk about everything."

"About God?"

"Well . . . no."

"About dreams?"

"Um . . . not usually."

"About death or life or mysteries?"

I felt cornered. I really liked Marta. She was friendly and fun and when we were alone together . . . wow! "You know, Icarus, not everyone goes around talking about that kind of stuff all the time. A lot of people don't even think about that kind of stuff much. That doesn't make them bad people."

"I didn't say Marta was bad, N."

"But you don't like her," I accused.

"I don't hate her," he said. "She's just kinda boring."

"Some people think you're boring. Did you ever think of that?"

"I don't care what people think about me. I don't care if they like me or not. I don't care if they understand me. And you're the one that brought it up."

"Get over yourself, Ben," I said, leaving him on the grass with infinite beams of light chasing through the sky. I called Marta on the phone and listened as she told me in minute detail about her trip to the mall with Tiffany and Kelsey.

BEN

Sharp bayonets of pain slashed at my back. Jumping up, I stripped off my shirt as I ran to the mirror.

Even before I saw my reflection, I felt my wings. I felt them tear through my flesh and unfurl. I guess it was innate, instinctual, because I knew right away what to do. I stretched and flittered my wings, shaking off the droplets of preemergent moisture clinging to their surfaces.

The feeling of pride and power and completeness that washed over me when I stood before the mirror and saw the shimmering magnificence of my reptilian wings was something I had anticipated since I was born. Those wings were beautiful. True dragon's wings—scarlet when the light caught them at one angle, and bright lizard green when the light caught them at another. They probably had a seven-and-a-half or eight-foot wingspan from wing tip to wing tip.

I opened the window and climbed out on the sill. The sky was littered with stars. They were summoning me. I jumped from the window and fell for a moment. Then my wings caught the air and I began to soar—up, up, up.

Flying felt even better than I had imagined it would. The instant I took to the air, I knew—as I had always known—that flying was my destiny, my identity, my conclusion.

Higher, higher, higher I soared. The sky was my kingdom, the stars my minions. I swirled and swooped and spiraled through the night until I saw the copper sun displacing the stars and the darkness.

That was when my ecstasy became fear. The sun melted my reptilian wings away, and I began cascading earthward, cartwheeling from darkness into light. Faster and faster and faster I tumbled as my nemesis, Gravity, pulled me down. I was screaming, and then N was standing over me, shaking me by the shoulders until I forced my eyes open.

"Wake up, Icarus, wake up," said N.

I looked up, finding myself on our living room sofa. "Was it only a dream, then, N?" I asked him.

"Only a dream."

I turned my face toward the wall. I felt a sense of betrayal and deep regret. I twisted my arm to rub it against my back. No wings. No scars. Only shame, grief, pain.

And Gravity was there, knowing his warning had been issued. Smug in the power of his grasp.

BEN

I sat with N, Marta, and Mary Catherine at a baseball game. Mason played center field, and Roy, Mary Catherine's brother, was pitching. It was obvious that Marta and Mary Catherine didn't have much regard for each other. Marta immediately asserted her ownership of N. She sat on the bleacher step in front of him, and leaned back against him, peppering her speech with "Ian sweetie," "honey," and "love." I think Mary Catherine was amused because she kept jabbing me in the ribs with her elbow and then we'd exchange smirks.

"There's Kelsey. I'll be right back," Marta said when she spotted her girlfriend approaching. She kissed N's mouth and pranced away.

"Hey, Stalker, did you ever consider getting your nose pierced?" Mary Catherine asked. To me, she was the coolest girl in the whole school. She wasn't afraid of anything. That day, she was doing her Jackie O. fashion thing. She had on a tailored little suit and a pillbox hat and was carrying a compact handbag. For a baseball game!

N looked puzzled. "Me . . . with a pierced nose? I don't think so!"

"Too bad—if you did, Marta could lead you around by the ring in your nose."

I couldn't help it. I started laughing. Mary Catherine laughed, too. We clutched our sides and slapped each other's shoulders.

N didn't laugh, though. He leaned over, propping his elbows on his knees, and suddenly became absorbed in a scoreless, uneventful baseball game.

BEN

"Icarus?"

I straddled my board at the lineup. A girl waved at me from a few yards away. She looked familiar, but I couldn't place her. As she paddled to catch a wave, I was definitely intrigued. I watched her rise on her board and slice through the water.

When I hit the shoreline after my set, the girl was sitting in the sand. It was the tilt of her head that gave her away. "Kaitlyn?"

I hadn't seen her since eighth grade. She still looked like herself, but this version was striking. If the Kaitlyn from middle school had been a block of raw marble, this one was the Venus de Milo.

"So Casey Jones, how are you doing?" she asked, referring to my sixth-grade History Fair role. I laughed. Looking at her sitting in the sand with sunlight falling all around her, I could barely connect her with the scrawny girl dressed in flannel and denim and lugging a sledgehammer during our presentation.

"I'm fine. What about you, John Henry?"

"Great!"

I sat beside her. "Guess you traded in your sledgehammer for a surfboard."

"Can't ride a sledgehammer," she replied dryly. "Not that I've actually tried."

The wind blew her hair away from her face. Her eyes reflected the ocean. We sat together on the beach, talking, catching up. I hated it when her friends approached saying it was time to go.

IAN

Ben and I were on the porch playing chess when Marta drove up in her Honda Civic. "Do you have plans with Marta?" he asked.

"I don't think so."

She parked but didn't get out. I walked up to her side of the car, and she rolled the window down. "Get in. We're going to the mall."

"We are?"

"Yes, Ian. Now, get in."

"Hang on." I walked back to the porch. "She wants me to go to the mall. Can we finish later?"

"Whatever." Ben looked disgusted. I knew he felt shafted.

"Sorry, Ben, but she'll get mad."

"So let her get mad."

"You haven't seen Marta when she's mad."

She blew the horn. One quick toot.

"Do you even want to go to the mall?" he asked.

"Not really. But . . . she knows I'm just sitting here, so if I say no she'll be pissed."

"She'll get over it. N, do what you wanna do. She doesn't own you."

She blew the horn again—a long blast.

"I'm off. Later, Icarus." I hopped from the porch and ran across the yard as she revved the engine.

"Took you long enough," she said coldly.

"Why don't we see if Icarus wants to come?"

She looked at me like I'd suggested eating from a Dumpster. "I know he's your brother, Ian, but he's so weird. I don't want him tagging along all day."

At the mall, we ran into a few of Marta's friends. They were all giggling and gossiping. I felt like a pet dog the way she glommed with them and left me on the periphery. I was watching some middle-school kids dragging their skateboards down the escalator when Marta turned to me. "Come on, we're going to the food court."

We pulled two tables together. "Ian, I want some French fries," she said, using her sweetie pie voice to get what she wanted. "And a soda."

As I stood in line, I watched Marta with her girlfriends. She really was sexy, and she sure knew how to move her body. But she wasn't all that nice. I thought about Sarah Quentin and how she had always been so real. Then it was my turn in line, and I brought Marta her food. She took it from me, sipped her drink, and turned to her friend Kelsey. "Want some?" Kelsey took the drink, and Megan, another girl, picked up a French fry. Every time I said anything, Marta looked at Kelsey and rolled her eyes.

On the way home, I said, "Marta, I don't know about us."

"What do you mean?"

"We don't seem to . . . um . . . be suited for each other."

She put on her blinker and pulled the car off the road. "Don't we?" she asked, unbuckling her seat belt. She slipped her hand behind my neck, pulled me toward her, and kissed me. I instantly forgot everything.

BEN

Mason slammed his locker. "You asked *who* out?"

"Kaitlyn."

"History Fair Kaitlyn? From middle school?"

"Yes."

"And she turned you down?"

"Yeah."

"Bummer . . . talk about role reversal."

"She did say I could call her—that she might go surfing with me."

"So did you call her?"

"Not yet. Mason, you wouldn't believe how fabulous she is!"

"I never thought I'd hear *you* say that about *Kaitlyn*."

"You shoulda seen her on her surfboard. She was so powerful. Not at all intimidated on the water. And she's amazing. Smart and funny in a dry way. She's beautiful, too. I can't get her out of my mind."

"Well, I always liked Kaitlyn. I never could figure out why she bugged you so much."

"Maybe I was scared or something. You know—not so much of her specifically, but of the idea of any girl-friend."

"You're interesting, Icarus. I've only known you to be scared of two things—girls, and Gravity!"

IAN

Ben came to me just when I finished changing the oil in the car. "You got a minute?"

"Sure. What's up?" I put the oil filter wrench back in the toolbox and wiped my greasy hands on a rag.

"I have a brainstorm."

My heart sank. Ben's brainstorms usually meant some outlandish scheme to cause his wings to emerge. I'd gotten to the point that I was weary of the whole flying thing. "Oh?"

"Yeah. Remember Aunt Anna talking about Mom's paintings?"

"Yeah."

"Don't you wish Mom still painted?"

"I guess."

"Let's get her some paints for her birthday."

"Huh?"

"Paints. I talked to Mrs. Isaacs at school. She told me what to get, but oil paints are expensive. I can't afford them on my own. But if you and Pop also contributed . . ."

"That's your brainstorm?"

"Yeah."

"It has nothing to do with wings."

He looked at me, puzzled. "Mom doesn't want wings, N."

"Right."

"So, whadda ya think? Do you like my plan?"

"Yeah, I do, Icarus. Count me in." I picked up the toolbox and the empty oil containers and headed for the barn.

So Ben, my father, and I went to the art supply store and bought paints, canvases, and various other artist paraphernalia. Ben untangled the easel from the jumble of debris in the dark side of the attic and brought it downstairs. We stuck a huge bow on it and wrapped the other things in bright paper.

When she saw what we had done, my mother's eyes sparkled with tears and she flashed us a huge smile. "This is truly a gift from the heart," she said as she hugged and kissed each of us.

When I came home from school a few days later, a rich, heavy smell permeated the house. My mother was in her studio (formerly the dining room) standing before her easel with a paintbrush in her hand. I watched her paint for several minutes before she became aware of my presence. She was that absorbed in her work.

When we sat on the porch eating Chinese takeout that evening, my mother smiled at us. Then she said, "Thank all of you for reigniting my dreams."

"Life's nothing without dreams," said Ben, looking into her eyes.

BEN

It took several phone calls and some urging to get Kaitlyn to see me.

"I'll meet you at the beach," she said. "Same place I saw you last time. One o'clock Saturday."

I got there early. She was a little late. I was afraid she wasn't going to show at all. She walked across the dunes with a sarong wrapped around her waist, her surfboard in her arms. "I forgot my board," I said. "We'll have to ride together."

"Forget it!"

"I was only kidding. It's over there."

She must have known she fascinated me. I couldn't take my eyes off her. We surfed a bit, but mainly we horsed around in the water or sat in the sand talking.

"You've changed a lot since middle school," she said.

"You, too."

Kaitlyn smiled. "I don't mean just physically. You act different. More confident. Less awkward."

"I wasn't awkward, was I?"

"That's putting it mildly! But so was I!"

I took her hand, and to my relief, she didn't pull it away. "I'm sure glad to know you again," I told her.

"You haven't scratched the surface," she said cryptically.

"Then you'll have to let me spend more time with you."

"Let's paddle out and catch that next set of waves."

"Does that mean you'll see me again?"

She winked, picked up her board, and stepped into the water.

IAN

Marta dumped me just before my graduation. She had big plans for the future, and they didn't include me. I couldn't say I was exactly heartbroken, but I did miss those nights with her. I hadn't really worked her into my long-term plans, but I'd sure thought we'd spend the summer together. Instead, I'd see her at parties turning on the charm for someone else while I stood alone in some corner or bunched with a crowd of rowdy guys.

BEN

It was late afternoon, and the sunlight filtered through the trees at a sharp angle so the shadows fell to the ground in bold stripes. "I wonder if Gravity pulls the shadows down," I said to Kaitlyn.

"You sure give Gravity a lot of credit. But no, I don't think so. 'Cause if the light source is on the ground, the shadows spread upward."

"Yeah, you're right. I didn't think about that."

"We're not gonna get lost, are we?"

"No . . . I've roamed these woods all my life . . . not that I'd mind getting lost in the woods with you!"

"Clever boy," she said playfully, and kissed me.

"Come here . . . look. I think it's a wood thrush's nest. I saw a pair of them here the other day."

"Do you come here a lot?"

"Yeah. I always have. See that tree . . . N and I used to pretend it was a wizard who'd been punished for using illegal magic. Look at all those bumps on the trunk—doesn't it look like the face of a wizard?"

"Hey, it does. That's wild."

"If you feed an acorn from that tree to a princess, the wizard gets released from the spell. That's the game N and I played. . . . Wanna eat an acorn?"

"Not really." She ran her fingers across the bark, studying the face of our wizard through touch. Suddenly she snatched her hand away from the tree. "Ouch . . . he bit me!" She laughed. I laughed with her, then took her hand and kissed her fingertips.

Mary Catherine slipped into the seat across from me. "How are you doin'?"

"Fine. You?"

"Great." She was dressed classily in Audrey Hepburn style, with a string of pearls around her neck and a simple black dress. Her dark brown hair was drawn up in a French knot. Suddenly I realized that I didn't even know what Mary Catherine's natural hair color was—since I'd known her, she'd sported a vast array. "But let's order quickly, because I have to be back at work in an hour."

"How's the job?"

"Right up my alley!" She'd been hired to work as a sales-girl at a bridal shop. She loved the fine fabrics and beautiful gowns.

"I always thought you'd go into some fashion field. I still can't believe you'll be majoring in marine biology."

"You're looking at the Crocodile Hunter of the future, 'cept I'll be wearing lace and velvet more often than he does!"

"With pearls?"

"Or diamonds. Depending upon the occasion! But since you brought up career choices, I still can't picture you as a computer geek."

"Did I say anything about geeks? I thought for sure I used the phrase *computer engineer.*"

"Which translates to geek, right?"

"Wrong!"

"So, Stalker, are you getting over Marta?"

"I'm over her."

"I still can't quite figure out what you were doing with her in the first place."

"Me either. Mental illness, I guess."

"You shoulda stuck with Sarah."

"I thought I was into that variety thing of yours."

"Doesn't work for everyone, Stalker. And now Sarah's off on a sailing trip . . ."

"I know. With her perfect boyfriend. Don't rub it in."

"Sorry. When are you leaving town?"

"About two weeks. School starts after Labor Day."

"You excited?"

"Yeah. . . . Sometimes I wish I was going local, like you, so I'd still be around here."

"They just happen to offer what I want here. Otherwise, I'd be long gone!"

BEN

Kaitlyn brought something new and special to my life. I could talk to her about everything, and she never made me feel frightening or delusional. It was like she understood me completely. Even so, there was a restless energy inside me, always reminding me that I had other promises—someone to become. A secret part of me always worried about my wings and my destiny. I found myself gravitating to my mother's studio. She was painting nearly every day, and she was pulsing with energy all the time.

I sat with her in her studio one night. The windows were open and I could hear the crickets outside. "Mom, watching you paint is like talking without words."

I guess that surprised her, because she put down her paintbrush and sat beside me on the floor. "You are so very special, Ben." She embraced me. Beneath the aroma of oil paint and turpentine, I smelled her sweet, clean scent.

I loved her studio—the organized chaos, the waves of creative energy, the dreams and memories revealed in the brushstrokes and colors on the canvases.

"So, Mom, I guess N's not coming back for a while?"

"Not till Christmas. It sure is quiet without him, isn't it?"

"Yeah."

She twisted her fingers in my curls like she did when I was little. "He's always been your best friend. Since the day you were born." I knew she was right, in spite of the occasional sibling wars between us. "It was like this when Ian started kindergarten, and you were home all day. You didn't even always want to play with him when he got home. You simply wanted him there."

I laughed. "Did I drive you crazy?"

"Not about that. But your wings . . . that was another matter." She recounted some of the outlandish things I'd done as a child. From the way she told them, I realized that she thought I'd outgrown my desire for wings. She was unaware of the longing in my heart and the itching at my back.

It was different with my father. He would watch me at times, like he was trying to read me. His eyes would be full of questions, but before I could answer them, he'd look away. I knew he feared I was unbalanced and dangerous. I just wished he understood that I didn't have a death wish. I simply wanted to realize my destiny.

BEN

I stood on the end of the diving board—my back to the water. It was the first meet of the school season, and I was pumped up for it. I knew Kaitlyn was in the stands, watching, and I really wanted to nail this dive. So far, I had performed well—better than ever before, and if I landed this last dive, I'd be in the running for top score. Really, though, I was more worried about impressing Kaitlyn than anything else.

I closed my eyes to compose myself, trying to clear my head. Then I moved so that only my toes rested on the board. I sprang up and flipped and twisted my way to the water's surface.

I knew it was a good dive. It felt right. When I emerged from the pool, I didn't look at the judges on their platform. I looked into the stands and found Kaitlyn's face. She smiled and gave me a thumbs-up.

"No wonder you think you'll sprout wings!" she said later. "You were sure flying off that diving board. It was beautiful to watch."

"I knew about my wings long before I learned how to dive," I replied.

"Well, maybe you won't get wings. Maybe diving's the sort of flying you're supposed to do."

"No. I'll get my wings. You'll see."

When I came home from college over Christmas break, I spent more time with Ben than I had in years. Either he had changed a whole lot, or being apart for several months had made me realize that my brother was no longer a little kid. He'd grown his hair long, and his body was hard and lean. But it was his eyes that were really different—like steel. They were further away somehow. It's hard to describe, but when I looked into them I wondered where Ben had gone and when he would be coming back.

Only when he was with Kaitlyn were his eyes soft and warm. It amazed me how connected he was to her. Even from across the room, I could feel the energy flow between them. I'd never really had that with a girl. Certainly not with Marta, maybe a little with Sarah, but not to that degree. Around Kaitlyn, Ben let down his guard in a way I hadn't seen since we were kids.

"Does Kaitlyn know about your wings?" I asked one day while we played cards at the kitchen table.

"Yeah."

"What's she say about all that?"

"She thinks it'll be great to fly."

"So she thinks you'll get them?"

"Um . . . well, she believes it could happen. She doesn't think I'm demented."

"And you're still waiting?"

He looked up. "For my wings? Yeah."

"It might never happen."

"It'll happen."

"Maybe you should just let it go, Icarus."

He put down his cards. "I can't do that."

"But you're wasting your life. You're so creative, so capable."

"You think I'm wasting my life?" His voice took on an edge.

I hated to say those things to him—I knew they hurt him—but I felt I had to. It was practically a moral responsibility. "Ben, lots of people want things they never get. Material things, spiritual things, emotional things, physical things . . . in your case, wings. You've got to move on at some point."

"Why?"

I didn't know what else to say. This whole obsession had worn me down. "Your turn," I said, sliding his hand of cards toward him.

BEN

Pop woke me up early one Saturday morning. "Ben, I'm going for a ride. I want to check on those new trees out on State Road Twenty-seven. I thought you might want to come along." When we were younger, N and I went with him a lot, but he hadn't asked me in a couple of years.

I forced my eyes open. It was still dark outside the window of my kingdom. Pop always liked to get an early start. "Yeah, okay." I rolled out of bed and grabbed a pair of shorts and a T-shirt.

By the time I made it downstairs, he'd poured me a cup of coffee. "Let's go." I followed him out the door to the truck—a white Ford F150 with the paper company logo tattooed on the doors.

Once miles of highway had passed by us, Pop turned onto a two-lane road. I saw large dew-draped spiderwebs woven into the overgrowth lining the highway. Other than a cumbersome logging truck that rumbled by and honked at us, we saw no one.

Pop took a left on a clay road. Towering pines were planted in straight rows on both sides. We drove for a few more miles, leaving a trail of red dust in our wake. Suddenly there was a break in the trees and we were embraced by the morning sun. The fields were planted with seedling pine trees that were about three feet tall. Pop pulled over and reached beneath the seat to retrieve his clipboard.

I walked beside him among the seedlings. He stopped now and then to make notes on his clipboard. He handled the seedlings as if they were his own children, often pausing to admire an exceptionally robust one.

After walking row upon row of pines, he led me into a thick grove of hardwoods. "This is actually park service land. It's beautiful, isn't it? When I'm out this way, I come here to eat my lunch." The ground dipped, and the trees thinned. He led me to a huge, flat boulder that overlooked a creek. "Right here. This is my special place." He sat, so I sat next to him.

"It's beautiful, Pop. And musical, too . . . the creek, the rustling leaves, the birds and insects . . ."

"I've been coming here for years. You're the only person I've ever brought. I thought you'd like it here."

I knew that he had given me a gift by sharing his place with me. I suddenly felt closer to him than I had in a long time. We sat together in silence, sharing the warmth of the sun and the concerto of the creek.

We walked back through the seedlings to the truck. "Where do you see yourself a few years from now, Ben?" Pop asked.

"Who knows? I don't even know where I'll be a few days from now."

"But surely you must have given some thought to your future. You've only got one more year of high school."

"The future is such a strange concept to me. I don't wanna plan my entire life now."

"No one thinks you should do that. But you could set some goals. Goals are flexible, Ben. You can change your mind. But you oughta be aiming for something."

Flexible? My one and only goal wasn't flexible at all. It was also one I knew not to share with him.

"When you go to college—"

I interrupted him. "I'm not going to college, Pop. I've told you that before."

"But you have so much ability, and there are endless possibilities for someone like you."

"Rich man, poor man, beggar man, thief . . . ," I said cynically.

"No. But you could be a naturalist or a zoologist. You could do research or fieldwork. You could be a park ranger—"

"I'm *not* going to college."

We drove to the paper company's annex office located in the forest. It was just an old trailer on cement blocks. Pop slipped the key into the lock and led me inside. It was hot and stuffy. "Miserable, isn't it?" Pop asked as he flipped on an antique oscillating fan, which simply stirred up the thick air. "We only turn on the air-conditioning if we're using the office all day. It takes forever to cool off this tin can." He walked to the bank of file cabinets against the back wall and removed a manila envelope. When he handed it to me, I saw that it was labeled BEN in big black letters. "Well, open it."

It felt heavy, and whatever was inside was oddly shaped and slightly bulky. Curious, I ripped off the flap. "A rock?" I dumped it into my hand.

"Turn it over." His eyes were expectant.

I picked it up with my other hand and examined it. At

first glance I missed it. The delicate imprint of some ancient dragonfly was etched into the flat side of the rock. A perfect fossil. I looked into Pop's eyes. "It's amazing. So flawless and complete. So much history and mystery. Where did you get it?"

"My special place—well, our special place now. I knew it was yours the minute I found it, but I wanted you to see where it came from first. That's part of the magic, don't you agree?"

"Yeah . . . so you're giving it to me?"

"Let's call it a gift from the earth, son. I'm just the delivery boy."

I marveled over that fossil for the entire ride home. The more I looked, the more I saw . . . the large head, the solid thorax, the slender abdomen, and the delicate, lacy wings. I fell into the life of that ancient insect; felt him flying in iridescent splendor over prehistoric landscapes. When we arrived home, I touched Pop's arm before he got out of the truck. "Thanks for sharing your special place, and the fossil, and everything."

"Thank you, Ben, for sharing those things with me."

I took the dragonfly up to my kingdom and placed it on the windowsill. I knew I would eventually draw it and write about it in my notebook. But not yet. I wanted to be fully acquainted with it first.

IAN

My father helped me get a summer job at the paper company. I never could have dreamed how much my life—our lives— would change that summer.

I worked all day in the yard at the plant. The heat was unbearable, the sun relentless, the humidity murderous. My hands blistered and bled at first, then became calloused. My skin darkened, but not like a surfer—like the laborer I was. I spent my breaks trying to cool off in the small trailer crammed with folding chairs and vending machines.

I could hardly pursue all of the summer pleasures I had fantasized about because of my exhaustion. My social life was zilch except for the occasional dinner with Mary Catherine. When I met her at our favorite haunt my first night home, she was more beautiful than ever. Her light brown hair was soft and shiny, curling gently around her face. Her brown eyes were fluid and clear. Throughout our meal, I puzzled over whose style she was currently mimicking. Finally, I asked her.

She smiled, cocked her head, and said, "I'm just me, Stalker! Mary Catherine! From now on, I'm just me!"

"I like you best this way."

"Thanks. I do, too."

Ben was working at a place on the beach, renting out surfboards, sailboards, kayaks, umbrellas, and beach chairs. He wore board shorts, shades, and a visor. His tan was much more golden than mine. He went swimming on his breaks. And—the clincher—he got paid better than I did.

Ben was spending most of his spare time with Kaitlyn or Mason and usually came home only to sleep or change clothes.

Then, one moonlit night, everything unraveled.

I picked Mason up from his job at the supermarket and drove to Kaitlyn's house.

"Where's the car?" I asked her when we got there.

"My parents are at a party."

"You didn't go?"

"To hobnob with the ancient wonders? Please! Let's play a game," suggested Kaitlyn, and she dragged the Trivial Pursuit game out of the closet. I was sure Mason would win—he always knew the answers on *Jeopardy!* and other quiz shows. We sat at the dining room table and spread out the game board.

After a few rounds, Mason got a question that should have been mine. Kaitlyn read it to him. "Who escaped from Minos's labyrinth by flying out?"

We all laughed, and naturally, Mason responded correctly. "Daedalus and Icarus."

I rose and bowed theatrically. "In the flesh!"

"But still wingless," laughed Mason.

"The time will come," I promised.

"While we're waiting, why don't you get me a drink?" Mason said.

"Me too," added Kaitlyn. "If you make some cheese sauce, that'd be good, too. There's a bag of chips on the counter."

"No problem," I said, walking past them into the kitchen. I'd hung around Kaitlyn's house enough to know my way around. After dumping the Tostitos into a bowl, I cubed the cheese and added salsa, then put it in the microwave to melt. I went to stand in the doorway while I waited. I didn't mean to eavesdrop, but I couldn't help it.

". . . sprout wings. But he believes it."

"But Kaitlyn, you know he's nuts."

"But harmlessly so. He'll outgrow it. In his heart, I'm sure he knows it's all a fantasy."

"He's stood by this so-called fantasy since I met him. Does he think you believe it, too?"

"I guess, in a way. But Mason, he's very imaginative. I don't think he's truly serious. It's just a sort of long-term game."

"He's as tenacious as a bulldog. It's what he believed when he was little, and he still won't let it go. He should. You know it. I know it. But no way I'm telling him. He's so defensive about the whole thing. He and Rico quit being friends when Rico laughed."

"It doesn't hurt to indulge him."

My throat was closing up and my hands clenched into fists. I felt betrayed and ridiculed. For years, Mason had led me to believe he had faith in my destiny, and Kaitlyn had done the same thing since we'd started seeing each other. But now, their words shattered me. I stepped into the room just as some distant part of me heard the microwave beep.

"Am I such a joke, then?" I asked, my voice quivering slightly. "Worth a few good laughs?"

They both looked at me, and I saw their faces flood with shame. "It's not like that," Kaitlyn protested. "Not at all."

She rose and took my arm, but I shook her off. "Don't touch me. It's all put on, isn't it? I thought you believed in me. Both of you. And now . . ."

"Icarus—" Mason began.

I cut him off. "Call me Ben. That other name is nothing but a taunt coming from you. You're mocking me."

Mason stood and took a step toward me. "You know we didn't mean anything. We're your friends—"

"Friends! You've been ragging on my dreams—the deepest, purest part of me. It's like I'm nothing. Less than nothing. I thought you believed in me, and all along . . ." I could feel the breakdown coming, but I refused to do it in front of them—to give them more fodder for their jabs. I turned, dashed through the kitchen and out the back door. Yanking the keys from my pocket, I wrenched the truck door open. As I backed out of the driveway and sped off, I saw Kaitlyn and Mason running down the steps after me. But I didn't stop.

IAN

I was sound asleep when the phone rang. I'd worked over-
time all week, grueling physical labor in heavy humidity and
under a blazing sun. I was so tired I felt drugged. "Hello?" I
glanced at the clock, its luminous numbers blazing through
the darkness of the room. 11:17.

"Ian?"

"Yeah?"

"It's Kaitlyn. I'm glad you answered. I don't wanna wake
up your parents. Is Ben there?"

I tried to shake off my vague dreams and catch her
words. "Ben?"

"Yes. He left here a few minutes ago."

"I'll check. Hang on." I looked out the window. My
father's truck, which Ben had borrowed for the night, wasn't
there. "Kaitlyn, he's not here yet. I'll have him call you when
he comes in."

"Ian . . . I'm scared. Icarus is—he's—I don't know what
to call it . . . irrational, I guess. He tore out of here a little
while ago."

"Huh? What's going on?"

"Icarus overheard Mason and me talking . . . about his wings. He heard us say we didn't really believe . . . we didn't mean for him to hear. But he freaked out. I've never seen him so angry. We didn't mean to hurt him, Ian. But you know how sensitive Icarus is about his wings. I don't know what to do. My parents have the car, so I can't go after him. And I don't know where he was going."

"Whoa! Calm down and tell me what he said."

"I dunno. Stuff about how we thought he was a joke. Which isn't true. I love Ben. I just don't get this obsession of his. We don't know what to do."

By now I was fully awake, and I was unsettled. Kaitlyn sounded totally rattled. "Where's Mason?"

"He's here, but like I said, we're stranded. And we're worried. Really worried."

"I'll go look for him, Kaitlyn. I'm sure he's fine."

"Call me when you find him. And Ian, tell him I want to see him . . . that I love him. I can't stand for him to think I've laughed at him. I haven't. He just misunderstood."

"I know, Kaitlyn. I've been dealing with it my whole life. I'll find him."

I flipped on the light and grabbed my shorts from the chair. I tried to think clearly. I knew Ben better than anyone else in the world. I didn't doubt that what he'd overheard had wounded him deeply.

I sat on the bed, my head in my hands. Where was he, I wondered.

A shadow passed over me. I looked up at my father standing in the doorway. "Who was on the phone?"

"Um . . . Kaitlyn. She was looking for Ben."

"He said he was going to her house tonight."

"Something happened."

"What?"

"I dunno. A fight, I guess. I'll go look for him."

"Look for him?"

"Don't worry, Pop. I'm sure everything's fine." I slipped on my flip-flops, grabbed my keys, and left.

It wasn't until I pulled out on the street that I knew where I was headed . . . where Ben was headed. I turned onto the highway and drove to the trestle.

BEN

The tires squealed as I raced around the corner. The things they had said . . . and me, the fool . . . always the fool.

No one believed in me. Not even N, though he tried to hide it—to be nice about it—even he didn't believe in me. And Mom and Pop sold me out before I was six. But Mason had always encouraged me when I told him about my wings . . . and Kaitlyn . . . Kaitlyn—I thought she understood. I believed that she loved me, when I was nothing but a caper to her—someone to laugh at, to belittle, to *indulge*.

The shame . . . the pain . . . all the years of being the pathetically delusional little boy . . . why couldn't anyone, anywhere, believe in me?

IAN

I saw Ben stalking across the gravel roadbed at the foot of the trestle. "Icarus," I called as I jumped from the car.

"What're *you* doing here?" His eyes were cold and wild.

"Funny, that's what I was about to ask you."

"Just leave." He spoke with frigid finality.

A shiver danced through me. "What are you gonna do?"

He didn't say anything, just looked at me. I'd never seen him so distant and removed.

"Ben, what's going on?" I grabbed his upper arm, but he pushed me away as if my touch had burned him.

"Ben, what are you gonna do?" I don't know why I asked, because I already knew.

"I'm gonna fly, N. That's what I'm gonna do."

"You're kidding, right?"

"Wrong."

"Ben, this is crazy."

"I didn't ask your opinion. I've heard it plenty of times already. And it's not crazy. It'll be the first sane thing I've done in a while. I'm sick of everyone thinking I'm some loser living in a dream world. And I'm sure sick of waiting around for my real life to begin."

"Please don't do this."

He started climbing the embankment. I knew I should try to stop him. I thought of our parents, and of the hole we'd have in our hearts and lives if something happened to Ben. But something about him was frightening me. Kaitlyn was right—I'd never seen Ben like that either.

So I followed him. Soon we were out over the water. I looked down at the diamonds of moonlight on the bay. No one was about. I saw no towboats with barges, no ships, no pleasure crafts.

The bridge ramped higher and higher above the water. It didn't bother Ben, but I felt a little queasy—the same way I'd felt when we were little and I climbed out on the roof with him.

"Are you scared, Ben?"

"Scared? Never! I've been wanting this all my life."

"But what if—"

"No *what-ifs*, N. And you can go on back to your safe happy ground-dwelling existence. I don't need an audience."

"I can't go. You know that."

He didn't respond. We climbed higher, nearing the center span. My heart was beating wildly—was it our height above the water, or the weight of what my brother was about to do? A yellow-crowned night heron swooped down in front of us and veered away, riding the wind.

"You can still change your mind, Ben."

"No, I can't. I made up my mind the day I was born. My big mistake was waiting this long. Indulging all of *you* and letting your fears influence my choices." He sounded bitter.

I could tell where dead center was because of the bright green light mounted there. As we approached it, Ben walked more slowly—like he was savoring the moment.

I caught up with him and touched his arm. "I love you,

Ben. That's why I'm not trying to stop you. But I'm scared to death."

He stopped walking. "Don't be." He stood before the light and kicked off his shoes. I looked over the rail. I couldn't believe how high up we were. Ben faced the water, then turned toward me. "N?"

"Yeah?"

"Whatever happens, I love you. And Mom and Pop. Always."

I felt tears in my eyes and blinked them back. We embraced. Then he stepped away, stripped off his clothes, and climbed onto the railing. I wanted to turn away, but to have done so would have been a betrayal.

He dove. He was graceful and acrobatic. But still, I watched in horror as Gravity took control. Down, down Ben fell. I expected to see him panic and snatch at the air, but he remained fluid and calm, slicing the night with his body. The water must have been miles away or time must have suspended itself. I grasped the railing tightly. My legs were trembling.

When a cloud smothered the moonlight, I noticed a thin layer of fog hovering at the water's surface. I hadn't seen it before. Had it been there? Ben slipped into the fog and I shivered, anticipating the sound of a splash. Helplessly, I called out his name as I stared into the fog.

A cry like a beast in pain shattered the night, and suddenly, Ben—no, Icarus—Icarus emerged from the fog, and the moon tossed off that cloud and showered him in its warm yellow light.

And I saw them—his wings. They were truly reptilian—brightly crimson at the wing tips, fading to orange and rich gold as they joined with his body. They reminded me of the fantastic dragons I remembered from the fairy tales we read as children.

BEN

It was the first truly complete moment of my life. What a rush it was to feel those wings busting out of my back—to feel them unfold and catch the wind. What power surged through me when I soared over the bay. What a thrill of pride I experienced when my reflection fell on the glassy surface of the water.

It made it all worth it—all that waiting, all those tears and nightmares, all of the skirmishes with Gravity. And when I soared through the air, Gravity was down there snarling at me—the dirty rotten ground-dweller that he was.

I felt so good, so strong, so pure. The moonlight on my skin—the wind in my hair—the sound of my wings—*my wings*—slipping through the air.

It was better than even my sweetest dream.

He soared and swooped and danced in the sky. He must have instinctively known how to use those wings, because from the moment they burst forth, he never wavered or fumbled. While I watched him, I felt tears on my cheeks, and the coolness left behind as the wind dried them.

Finally he landed beside me, folding his wings against his back. His eyes shone brightly, and his smile was dazzling. He grabbed me and hugged me tight.

"Icarus, my brother," I said.

"N, it was great. It was perfect. It was heaven!" He was so exhilarated.

I touched his wings—slender flexible bones encased in flesh textured with tiny scales like the skin of a green garden lizard, the colors rich and iridescent. "Icarus, I'm sorry. I'm sorry for not believing," I said, looking into his eyes.

"It's all right, N. That first time on the trestle, I knew my wings were ready. But the railroad guard stopped me, and maybe I lost some confidence after that, or maybe I let everyone else hold me back, but it was inevitable. I knew that even then." He shook his head. "I just regret that I waited so long."

Before I could respond, I heard shouts.

"Ben! Ian!" I saw our parents rushing toward us. My father must have reflected on Ben's history and known where we'd be.

"Thank God you're both safe," our mother said as they reached us.

Ben stood before them and extended his wings.

BEN

My parents didn't know what to make of my metamorphosis. They gaped at me, mute. Mom's eyes flooded with tears.

N broke the silence. "Ben got his wings," he said softly.

"So I see," Pop replied slowly, shifting his eyes to some distant place on the horizon.

I stepped in front of him, forcing him to look at me. "Pop, I'm happy, really happy, for the first time in my life. That's what you always said you wanted."

He met my eyes. "It is, son. But I never imagined this. How could I?" He reached out, stroking my left wing pensively. "Benjamin, what happens now?"

"I'll do what I've always said I would do. I'm going away."

My mother grasped my forearm. "You can't leave," she cried. "You're still so young. You'll be all alone."

"No, Mom, I won't. I'll find them—the others like me. Anyway I can't stay. I don't belong here anymore. Not now. Maybe someday I can come back."

N took my side. "We've doubted Ben his whole life—it only seems right to believe in him now."

My father nodded. "It's not easy to let you go, Ben," he said, placing a trembling hand on my shoulder. "It'll be the hardest thing I've ever done. But because I can see that you need to . . ." His voice broke. He wiped his eyes with the back of his hand. "Please be safe. Don't fly too high. Too far. Please."

My mother threw her arms around me and said, "I love you, Icarus."

I left, using the blanket of darkness to shelter me from scrutiny. I wished I'd had time to tell Mason and Kaitlyn—especially Kaitlyn—goodbye. I was afraid, though, that she might try to stop me from leaving, and for her, I just might have stayed. A few tears slipped from my eyes as I flew away. I was leaving the world I knew to search for one I'd always dreamed of.

When I told Mason and Kaitlyn about Ben's wings, they were overcome. Kaitlyn's face lost all color. "And he's gone?" she whispered.

"Gone."

"But where?"

"I don't know. Even he didn't know."

"But Ian, he couldn't just leave, could he?"

"He had to. It tore him up to go. Especially to leave you, Kaitlyn. He loved you. But he couldn't stay, either."

"He always said he would fly away when he got his wings, but I never believed it would really happen." She began to cry. I held her in my arms.

Mason looked at the horizon. "I feel like such a traitor. He was my friend, and I let him down."

"He understood. He knew how hard it was for all of us to—to accept his destiny."

"But Ian, we didn't accept it."

"No. But Mason, we accepted him."

IAN

I sat alone in the Kingdom of Icarus. I missed my brother. Inside me was the fear that I might never see him again. I regretted the words I'd never spoken—the dreams I'd never shared. I sat at his table, his shrine, and paged through his notebooks. It had been many years since I had looked at them. I was again struck by the quiet beauty and eloquence of both his drawings and his words. By the way he was able to capture the magic of small, simple things.

I could see tiny particles of dust suspended in the soft yellow light spilling through the window of his kingdom. A kingdom whose king had exiled himself in search of some new realm.

I stayed there for hours, touching things, watching the chandelier crystals in the window spark rainbows of light on the walls and floor. Watching those da Vinci wings stand guard.

ABOUT THE AUTHOR

Julie Gonzalez has a bachelor's degree in elementary education. She lives in Pensacola, Florida, with her husband, Eric, and their four children. *Wings* is her first young adult novel.

Finally I climbed down the stairway to heaven and closed the trapdoor. I pulled four thumbtacks out of the closet wall and took Icarus's NO GRAVITY sign with me. I hung it on the wall of my dorm room. Friends would ask me why it was there and what it meant. All I ever said was "Gravity is a powerful enemy, and don't you forget it."